THE OFFERING

THE BLACK ROOM MANUSCRIPTS
VOLUME ONE

GOD BOMB!
KIT POWER

Mr. Robespierre
Daniel Marc Chant

HORROROBOROS

THE EXCHANGE
J. R. PARK

AIMEE BANCROFT AND THE SINGULARITY STORM
DANIEL MARC CHANT

INTO FEAR
DANIEL MARC CHANT

KING CARRION
RICH HAWKINS

ONE GIRL ARMY
DANIEL MARC CHANT

PAUL KANE
DEATH

LYDIAN FAUST
FOREST UNDERGROUND

MAD DOG
J. R. PARK

HALLOWEEN NIGHT
a short story by J. R. Park

DEATH DREAMS IN A WHOREHOUSE
J. R. PARK

SINISTER HORROR CARDS
Sinister Horror Company

A Pocket Guide To The Sinister Horror Company

MONSTERS ARE REAL
RICH HAWKINS

SALVATION IS DAMNATION
HELL SHIP
BENEDICT J. JONES

THE BLACK ROOM MANUSCRIPTS
VOLUME FOUR

Featuring Stories and Articles by:

Daniel Marc Chant   Kayleigh Marie Edwards   Lydian Faust

Duncan P. Bradshaw   Mark Cassell   Chris Kelso

J. R. Park   Andrew Freudenberg   Kit Power

Tracy Fahey   Tim Clayton   Jonathan Butcher

Greetings mortals and welcome to the Sinister Horror Company Annual. You hold in your hands a tome of torment; a collection created at the very edge of sanity. Within these pages lurk nightmares made real, pulled from the psyches of some of horror's most talented & twisted minds. We present this offering to you as we lead you down the darkest paths. Enjoy, mortals, and fear for your flesh, for the shadows view you with greedy eyes.

Cernunnos
by Daniel Marc Chant

The call that cut short Detective Inspector Lydia Brooks' vacation came in at 0832 hours. There'd been a suspicious death in Saighir Village and they needed her there as soon as possible.

In a way, she was glad. After only a few days, London had already lost its allure. Next time she wanted to go somewhere noisy and expensive, she told herself, she'd go to Beirut. At least there she'd get a tan.

Displaying what she considered a healthy disregard for traffic laws, she arrived at Saighir Village in record time. The sight of its thatched cottages and quaint shops improved her mood to no end. She wasn't even put out at having to stop to allow a mother duck and her brood to cross the road.

Lydia drove on past the Norman church and the village green where a game of cricket was underway and came at last to the scene of the putative crime. Although Cowan Cottage was no bigger than most cottages in the village, its grounds were large enough to incorporate an ornamental pond and an apple orchard. Five cars were parked in the driveway. Lydia recognised four of them, which presumably meant the fifth belonged to the victim. It was an SUV – the sort of vehicle Lydia despised.

As she pulled into the driveway, a cloud of steam floated up from beneath the hood of her car, causing her heart to sink. She hoped nobody would notice. The last thing she needed was some patronising flatfoot telling her, 'It's your manifold, love'. So she quickly killed the engine and headed for the front door. It opened just as she reached it.

'Morning, ma'am,' said Sergeant Steele, touching the peak of an imaginary cap. Holding the door open, he stepped aside to allow Lydia in. 'You're going to like this one.'

Lydia couldn't help but give a slight shake of her head. It was the way she reacted nearly every time Steele opened his mouth. Despite knocking on 30, he was inclined to act like a teenager and to make asinine remarks. As usual, his slightly too small uniform was in dire need of being ironed. 'I should be on holiday,' she retorted, her tone making it very clear she wasn't about to like anything. 'Where's the body?'

'This way, ma'am.'

'Stop calling me ma'am. I'm a detective inspector – not a bloody school teacher.'

'Yes, ma'am.'

Resisting an urge to kick him where it would hurt most, Lydia followed Steele into the surprisingly spacious living room. It was crawling with policemen in a way that made her think of maggots inhabiting a corpse. 'Anyone who doesn't need to be here – out now. Go on. Scram.'

Making no attempt to hide their resentment, the cops shuffled out, leaving the room to Lydia, Steele and Roger Fleetwood, the police medical examiner.

Fleetwood had made himself at home in an armchair and was busy doing the Times crossword. He waved briefly to acknowledge Lydia's presence then carried on as if he were at home.

Lydia cast a quick eye around the room. It was expensively furnished, mostly with antiques. A large television and a stereo system seemed to be the only concessions to modernity.

The first thing that caught her interest was a skull – clearly not human - sitting on the oak desk next to a small forest of empty beer bottles. She was about to make a comment about it when she noticed the pile of ashes on the chair in front of the skull. A crate of beer on the floor beside the chair obscured her view of something she could just about see the edge of. Closing in, she found herself looking at a slipper full of ashes.

Sergeant Steele wore a smug expression. Lydia knew he was dying to say *I told you you were going to like this one*, so she quickly treated him to a look that said, Don't you dare.

Steele took the hint and said, 'Meet the late Donald Haig. Male, Caucasian. Mid-50s. Weight: approximately 140 pounds. Height: just under 6 foot. Hair: grey.'

Despite herself, Lydia was almost impressed. 'You can tell all that from a pile of ashes?'

'From CCTV footage. There are cameras on the roof. They show Mr Haig entering the cottage and nobody coming out. Ergo: this must be Mr Haig.'

'What happened to him?'

Roger Fleetwood looked up from his crossword, scratched the side of his nose with his biro and said, 'Spontaneous human combustion.'

On the last day of his life, Donald Haig went for a walk in the woods. His therapist had promised it would do him a world of good, both physically and mentally, but he wasn't in it for his health. He'd moved to Saighir Village with the intention of becoming a country squire and had a notion that going for long walks was part of that particular lifestyle. So every day he'd spend an hour or two traipsing around the countryside in his tweed jacket and matching cap.

As he came to a small stream, he had a feeling of being watched. It brought about a momentary attack of paranoia that caused him to duck and almost run for cover. But the feeling quickly passed and he laughed inwardly at himself. What was he thinking? That he was about to be torn apart by a lion? Here in the English countryside where the most vicious thing he was likely to encounter was a mosquito?

The snapping of a twig caused him to turn his head. Brown eyes regarded him through the foliage. They were inquisitive, intelligent, and seemed to be asking him what he was doing in the wood. Although they showed no hint of belligerence, he would not have called them gentle. Rather they seemed to be the eyes of something that wanted no trouble but knew how to deal with it should it have to.

The stag stepped out of the undergrowth. Impressed with its majesty and strength, Haig turned slowly, careful to show he presented no threat. This was as close as he'd been to a wild creature in a long time and he was as thrilled as he was wary.

He couldn't help himself. The predatory instincts that had made him a successful stockbroker caused him to point an imaginary rifle at the stag. Closing one eye, he aimed for the creature's forehead and squeezed his trigger. 'Kapow!'

The stag blinked. A look of disdain seemed to settle on the creature's face as it moved on, leaving the path and disappearing back into the undergrowth.

Haig felt cheated. If he'd had a real gun, he would now be the proud owner of a genuine – albeit illegal – hunting trophy.

For a brief moment, he contemplated buying a shotgun and going after the stag, but a better idea occurred to him. He would buy a stag's head and hang it on his wall. And if anyone asked if he'd killed the beast himself, he would look them in the eye and say yes.

'Spontaneous human combustion?' Lydia snorted her contempt.

'It's where a person bursts into flames with no apparent reason,' said Roger Fleetwood, putting aside his newspaper and lifting himself out of his chair.

'I know what it is, thank you very much. I also know there's no such bloody thing.'

'And yet here it is.' Fleetwood walked up to Lydia and put on a pair of half-rim glasses. He squinted at the chair. 'To reduce a human body to ashes like this takes a temperature close to 3,000 degrees centigrade. And yet the chair our incinerated pal was sitting in has one or two minor scorch marks and that's it. From which we can conclude that whatever caused Mr Haig to turn into a human bonfire came from within rather than without.'

'Assuming this is Mr Haig. How can we be certain these ashes are even human?'

'Right now, we can't. We'll know for sure once we've run some tests.'

Lydia turned to Sergeant Steele. 'I want this cottage searched thoroughly.'

'Already been done.'

'Then do it again. And this time look out for secret passages, priest holes or anywhere else Donald bloody Haig might be hiding. If he's making a fool of us, he's going to regret it big time.'

With a shrug, Steele left the room and began shouting orders to have the cottage gone over with the proverbial fine tooth comb.

Lydia turned her attention to the skull. 'What's this?'

'A skull,' said Fleetwood.

'I can see that. But the skull of what?'

'A stag, if I'm not very much mistaken. Minus the antlers, of course.'

'So what's it doing sitting on this desk?'

'You're the detective. You tell me.'

The shop was small and dingy. It smelt of damp, dust and other things Donald Haig didn't much care for. Since moving to Saighir Village, he'd passed it just about every day without giving it much thought. According to the sign over the doorway, it was an antiques emporium, but Haig had it marked down as an overpriced junk shop and would never have set foot in it but for his encounter with the stag.

A quick glance around the gloomy interior was almost enough to make him walk right out again. The place was filled with old furniture that had seen better days and curios that no one in their right mind would wish to purchase.

A picture on the wall caught his attention. It was an oil painting of folk in peasant garb performing what was clearly a pagan rite of some sort. They were gathered in a woodland clearing, dancing around a fire in front of which stood an effigy that appeared to be made of twigs and bones held together with tar.

What fascinated Haig about the picture was what the effigy was wearing on its head: a skull replete with antlers.

'May I help you?'

The voice startled Haig. He hadn't seen its owner – an old man wearing a velvet smoking jacket – come in.

The old man stood behind the counter looking every bit as much an antique as anything in the shop. 'Are you interested in purchasing that painting? I can do you a very good deal.'

'Actually,' said Haig, 'I'm looking for a stag skull.'

'You are?' The old man seemed surprised. 'I'm afraid I can't help you on that one.'

'Oh, well. It was a long shot.' Haig decided to leave before the old man tried foisting on him something he didn't want. As he headed for the door, he came upon a glass cabinet. Its contents stopped him in his tracks. 'What's that?'

'That?' said the old man, without even looking. 'That's just junk. I've been meaning to throw it out.'

'Looks like a stag skull to me.'

'Perhaps it is, but without the antlers it's worthless.'

'I'll take it.'

'I'm afraid it's not for sale.'

'A hundred quid.'

'I beg your pardon?'

'You heard. A ton.'

'As I say: it's not for sale. Not at any price.'

'I'm offering you a lot of money for something you just said is worthless.'

The old man shrugged his boney shoulders and went up in Haig's estimation. No stranger to haggling, he knew when he was being played and right now he was being played as well as he'd ever been. Common sense dictated that he leave the shop immediately and track down what he wanted elsewhere, but he was in no mood for rationality. If he wanted something badly enough, he was always prepared to pay over the odds, and right now he wanted the skull in the glass case as badly as an addict needs cocaine.

He held up his arm and pulled back the sleeve of his jacket. 'You see this watch?'

'Not from here.'

Haig marched up to the counter. 'See it now?'

The old man bent forward. 'Vintage Rolex. Do you mind if I... ?' He placed his ear to the watch. 'Oh, yes. That's the real thing all right.'

'Of course it's the real thing.' Haig deftly removed the watch and dangled it in front of the shopkeeper's face. 'Yours for that skull.'

Haig was pleased with himself. The fact that he'd paid way too much for the skull didn't bother him in the least. He'd got what he wanted and there were plenty more Rolexes in the world.

There was, in his book, only one thing to do after closing a deal like this, and that was to celebrate. In the past, that would have involved cocaine and other illegal substances, but not any more. Having seen many of his colleagues destroyed by drugs, it was a source of constant amazement to him that he'd made it to the end of his career without suffering the same fate.

I am one lucky bugger, he told himself as he placed the skull on the table in his living room. Seems like I can get away with anything.

With narcotics being off the menu, he went to the kitchen and brought back a crate of Old Growler Premium Bitter, a local beer he'd started drinking as part of his drive to fit in.

The two pubs in the village served Old Growler and whenever he went into one of them he made sure the locals saw him drinking it. He didn't want them to see him as some ponce from the City flouncing around with his fancy City ways. The sooner they accepted him as one of their own, the better.

So he drank Old Growler despite the fact he didn't really like the stuff. It had far too much flavour for his taste, but he was determined to get used to it.

Sitting down at the table, he aimed a remote control at his state of the art stereo system and hit the on button. His flat screen television came to life and offered him a menu of over a thousand acts starting at Aerosmith and ending with ZZ Top. Now what was it to be? He fancied something retro, something that had stood the test of time and was unarguably classic. The Beatles? No. Too obvious. Chuck Berry? Getting closer.

'David Bowie,' he decided and almost instantly changed his mind. Instead he selected the Rolling Stones and what he considered their greatest album – Beggar's Banquet. As the opening strains of Sympathy for the Devil issued from telephone box sized speakers standing like sentinels either side of the ornamental fire place, a sense of almost transcendental calm descended on Haig.

He took a gold plated bottle opener from his pocket, grabbed a bottle of Old Growler and opened it. Life, he told himself, doesn't get any better than this.

Sergeant Steele ambled back into the living room. 'There's some old geezer outside. Says that there skull belongs to him and he'd quite like it back.'

'Oh, does he?' Lydia felt her hackles rise. 'Tell him to fill out a claim form at the nick. Right now, that skull's not going anywhere.'

'He also says there's a curse attached to the skull.'

'That's all I bloody need.' Lydia pictured the headline in tomorrow's Saighir Chronicle: Village Resident Struck Down by Ancient Curse. Somewhere in the story, her name would almost certainly crop up, leaving everyone to assume she believed in the curse. Something similar had happened when she'd investigated a so-called Satanic blood sacrifice which turned out to be a pigeon killed by a fox; she wasn't about to let it happen again. 'An old man, you say?'

'He didn't give his name. Says he owns the antiques shop down Southside Road.'

'I suppose I'd better go talk to him then.'

By the time Haig had finished his second bottle of Old Growler, he'd decided it was the perfect accompaniment to the Rolling Stones. After all, what could possibly be more English than the Rolling Stones and beer the colour of ditch water served at room temperature?

With a satisfied belch, he cracked open a fresh bottle and poured it into his glass. As he did so, it occurred to him that the deer skull was a better, more fitting drinking receptacle. Isn't that what big game hunters did? Drink a celebratory drink from their victim's skulls?

As much as the idea appealed to him, he decided to forego the pleasure for now. Before his lips went anywhere near the skull, he was going to have it thoroughly disinfected. Then he was going to invite friends around and have them drink from the skull as a way of acknowledging kinship.

Friends? He chuckled at the thought. What friends? Before he became a stockbroker, he'd had quite a few friends, mostly old school chums he'd known for half his life. But as their lives diverged and they all settled down to mediocrity while he made a name for himself in the City, he'd cast them adrift one by one almost without noticing, and replaced them with a different kind of friend.

By the time he started thinking about getting out of the rat race, he had friends galore. Friends at the office. Friends in business. Friends in the City. Friends eager to spend his money and abuse his hospitality and stab him in the back for the sake of a quick buck.

When he announced his retirement, they threw him a lavish party, shook his hand, thanked him for this and that, and told him not to be a stranger. They reacted with enthusiasm when he invited them to visit him in Saighir Village any time they liked. 'We'll be down as soon as we can,' they lied. 'We'd hate to lose touch.'

And that was it.

No phone calls. No emails. Not so much as a card on his birthday.

'Bunch of bastards.' He took a healthy swig of Old Growler. Smacking his lips, he wondered why he hadn't gotten into real ale before now. So much better than that gassy piss-water called lager.

He decided to get drunk.

'The skull,' said the shopkeeper, 'is older than you think. It belonged to the Druids who lived here in the days before the Romans came. That was a time when the people lived peacefully and in accordance with Nature.'

'I don't give a flying monkey's how old it is,' Lydia responded. Now she was outside with fresh air in her lungs, she realised how unpleasant the air inside the cottage had been, carrying with it as it did the faintest hint of compost and stagnant water. 'The skull is part of an on-going police investigation. When we're done with it, we'll see it's returned to its rightful owner.'

'I advise you, dear lady, to hand it over before it harms anyone else.'

'And I advise you to get lost before I stick some handcuffs on you.'

'Please. I implore you. You don't know what you're dealing with here.'

Lydia's stomach grumbled, reminding her that she'd skipped breakfast. 'You have ten seconds to get off this property before I arrest you.'

'Very well,' said the shopkeeper. 'I've tried to warn you. What follows is on your own head. May the gods have mercy on you.'

When Beggar's Banquet finished playing, Haig decided on a bit of Bowie after all. Although he considered The Rise and Fall of Ziggy Stardust and the Spiders from Mars to be a seminal work of art, he much preferred Aladdin Sane, the album that came after it. Critics and fans alike seemed to regard Aladdin Sane as being slightly inferior to Ziggy Stardust, but so what? When they had a music system like his, then they could voice an opinion. Until then they could kiss his rich, successful butt.

As the intro to Watch that Man kicked in, he allowed himself to fantasise that Bowie was singing about him and for him. Donald Haig might be retired, but he wasn't about to go away. If the people of Saighir Village didn't want to embrace him, that was their look out.

For a while, he'd thought about abandoning his plan to buy the whole village and turn it into a holiday resort for the rich and selfish. But the way he'd been treated since arriving had strengthened his resolve. Buying Cowan Cottage had proven easier – and cheaper – than he'd expected, and he could see no reason why he couldn't acquire the rest of the village within a year.

Of course, the villagers would fight him tooth and nail, but he knew how to deal with people who got in his way.

'Bloody yokels. They'll be better off in tower blocks. This place ought to belong to people who appreciate the finer things in life.'

The room swayed gently. Haig gripped the edge of the table and grinned. The beer was going to his head and he liked the sensation. In the past he'd tried all sorts of chemical aids to help him relax and feel happy, but nothing compared to a bottle or two of Old Growler.

He pushed at the stag skull with his finger, causing it to spin a couple of times before coming to a wobbly stop. Tomorrow he would hire a craftsmen to mount it on a suitable base and attach it to the wall.

For want of anything better to do while he got drunk listening to David Bowie, he tipped some beer from his glass into the skull. There was a slight hiss as the froth settled to expose the bronze liquid beneath. The winking lights of his stereo system were reflected on the surface of the beer, allowing him to fancy he was looking into a pool full of nymphs or whatever it was that lived in water and glowed.

The level of the beer dropped noticeably. Haig put his hand on the table, expecting it to land in a puddle of ale.

The table was dry.

He leaned forward and tried to work out where the beer was going. There was no sign of it reaching the table and the outside of the skull looked and felt dry.

Soon there was no beer in the skull. He ran his finger tips over the inside of the cranium and noted with wry amusement that it was as dry as a bone.

'Well, blow me down.' The skull must have absorbed the beer, leaving behind not a single trace. He couldn't see how such a thing was possible, but then he'd never claimed to be a scientist.

The skull went out of focus. He blinked and it came back into focus surrounded by a haze of light.

Being no stranger to intoxication, the sight neither alarmed nor perturbed him. After so much beer, it was to be expected and a sure sign he was having a good time. Feeling suddenly playful, he turned the skull right side up and leaned forward to whisper in the hole that had once been its ear. 'You and me, buddy: we're going to take over the world.'

He leaned back and stared at the eye sockets. They seemed to stare back with unexpected malevolence. Beyond them lay shadow which seemed to pulsate as if crawling with thousands of tiny organisms. And though he thought it unlikely, he was certain he could make out his reflection in the darkness.

Some perverse inner compulsion made him want to dip his fingers into the shadow, but he was forestalled by a sudden dread. As his hand hovered over the skull, the shadow shifted and begin to ooze out of the sockets and drip down onto the table.

It was at that point that he decided he'd had quite enough to drink. Maybe if he'd thought to eat before going on his binge, he'd be all right. Now it would be all he could do to make it to the sofa to sleep off the Old Growler.

'Enough!' he cried, slamming his bottle onto the table. He tried to stand but his legs failed him. 'Bugger.'

The darkness kept pouring from the eye sockets. It seeped beneath the skull, pushing it ever upwards, forming a black column about two feet wide. Haig recalled a film he'd seen in a biology class many years ago. It was a time lapse recording of slime mould, which (if memory served) was a mass of single celled organisms that would from time to time come together to form a multicellular structure.

Was that what he was seeing now? Billions of microbes acting as one? It was as close as he could get to a rational explanation and he was determined to hang on to it for as long as he could.

When the column had risen high enough for the skull to be almost touching the ceiling, it stopped its upwards progress and grew outwards to twice its width. For a while, it quivered like a jelly, causing Haig to fear that the ungainly edifice was about to collapse on top of him. But it held firm and became still.

As Haig studied it, he was forced to discard his slime mould hypothesis, for the black mass was filled with what looked like random junk. As well as twigs, leafs, moss and tree bark, he could make out bones, teeth, ears, lips, veins and a host of other animal organs.

With a plop that made Haig picture a champagne bottle being de-corked, the column sprouted appendages near its apex. They protruded horizontally like branches on a tree. Five small columns germinated from the end of the appendages. As he formed the thought that the smaller appendages looked like fingers, the ones that might be branches bent upwards at right angles then flopped down to dangle at the sides of the column.

With another plop, the column's lower half split and moulded itself into two legs.

Haig's mind flipped back to the picture in the antiques shop and the effigy in front of the fire. It seemed the damn thing had found its way into his cosy cottage and was standing on his table. All that was missing were -

'Damn!' Haig was more annoyed than surprised to see a pair of antlers suddenly blossom from the skull. All he wanted was a few hours listening to music and abusing his liver, and what did he get? A bloody tar monster! Angrily, he jumped to his feet and gave the monster a mighty push which had no effect whatsoever.

As he sat back down, a voice spoke to him. 'Mortal, why doest thou disturb my rest?'

Haig looked up at the skull. His heart seemed to come to a juddering halt; for a long moment, he was unable to breathe. Things were getting out of hand, and for a control freak that was close to intolerable. It's an hallucination, he told himself. Your brain conjured it up; your brain can make it go away.

His heart leapt back into action and he was able to breathe again. As he exhaled, he pointed a trembling finger at the apparition and said, 'Get lost, you abomination!'

The tar monster shimmered. Haig sensed anger and contempt radiating towards him, and he immediately regretted opening his mouth.

'Freak?' Putting his hands on his hips and bending down like an adult confronting a naughty child, the tar monster spoke in measured tones. 'Hold thy tongue, mortal, lest I rip it from your mouth.'

Haig swallowed hard. He wanted to tell his unwanted guest to go to Hell, but the very thought of what might follow caused his stomach to contract. As much as he believed he was being threatened by a figment of his own imagination, there was a part of him that wasn't so sure.

Straightening up, the tar monster looked around the room. 'This be Joseph Wyatt's abode.'

'No.' The single syllable escaped Haig's lips as a coarse whisper. 'Mine.'

'Aye. That it might be, Joseph Wyatt being dead one hundred winters or more. Thee then must be the current master of Cowan Cottage.' The tar monster paused in expectation of a response which, due to his mouth being dry, Haig was unable to supply. Losing patience, the apparition roared, 'Speak, mortal!'

'Yes,' Haig squeaked. He took a quick swig of Old Growler and found his voice and his courage once more. 'I am Donald Haig. Who the hell are you?'

'I am that which I was and will always be. Throughout the centuries, I have had many names. When your ancestors lived in caves, I was known as the Monarch of the Hunt. When they learnt to farm the land, they called me the Spirit of the Harvest. These days, I am most commonly addressed as Cernunnos.'

'So what are you? A god?'

'To those who wouldst have me as a god, a god I am.'

'You think a lot of yourself, don't you?'

'In the presence of one such as thyself, why wouldn't I? Thy life is but a blink of an eye to me. I roamed this land in the days before Man and here I shalt be when thee and thy kind are but a memory.'

'Is that meant to impress me? Because I have to tell you, it ain't working, pal.' Feeling a surge of machismo, Haig opened a fresh bottle of Old Growler with his teeth and spat the top at Cernunnos. It disappeared into the creature's leg. 'I've had enough of this. I'm going to bed.' Haig got to his feet and felt the floor shift beneath him. With one hand resting on the back of the chair, he stood still until he was sure of his balance. When he was half certain he could at least make it to the door without falling over, he began the short but hazardous journey, laboriously placing each step with the greatest of care.

'Thou shalt stay,' said Cernunnos. Though his tone was soft, it conveyed all manner of threats. 'We are not done yet.'

'Wanna bet?' Hands at the ready to catch himself should he fall, Haig took another step and was preparing for yet another when he was arrested by a sound that reminded him of the rustling of autumn leaves. Something dark flowed from beneath the skirting board on all sides of the room. It crept towards him, a sphincter of menace constricting around his feet.

Instinctively he kicked out at whatever it was. It momentarily retreated before coming back at him amidst a fluttering of wings.

Aghast, he realised he was surrounded by cockroaches.

Bile rose in his throat. There was nothing on God's earth he hated more than cockroaches and the germs they carried.

Well, they weren't going to stop him going to bed. In fact, he relished the thought of walking across them, crushing their vile bodies beneath his feet.

Determinedly, he started for the door again. As he raised his foot, a legion of cockroaches rose up before him, but could not shake his resolve. He swatted at the creatures and took a step forward.

The cockroaches attacked. They were suddenly all over him, crawling up his arms and over his face. He spat some from his lips, snorted a few from his nostrils. He felt them creeping into his ears and down the front of his trousers.

Brushing frantically at his face, he was unable to stop them covering his eyes. He grabbed a fistful and squeezed the life out of a dozen of them.

He staggered back. His leg brushed against the chair and the next thing he knew he was sitting down and the cockroaches were retreating, dropping from his body and scurrying back to the skirting boards. Haig had no doubt they'd be back should he attempt to leave the room again.

'Ah, yes,' said Cernunnos. 'Thy ancestors had another name for me: Lord of the Cockroaches.'

Haig shivered as a fever came upon him and recognised that he was in shock and might very well faint. 'What do you want from me?'

'That which is mine to take.'

'The cockroaches? They're all yours. You can have them and all the other creepy-crawlies in this dump. First chance I get, I'm having this place fumigated.'

'Like many of thy kind, thou knowest not of that which matters. Greed is thy master. In its name, thou wouldst destroy that which is good, that which is right and in accordance with nature.

'I see what lies in thy mind. It is filled with dark thoughts and hatred. Thou wouldst take this village from its rightful owners. You wouldst destroy that which generations have built and fought for.

'I am Cernunnos, Monarch of the Hunt, Spirit of the Harvest, Lord of the Cockroaches, Defender of Saighir. And you, Donald Haig, are no more!'

Haig's fever intensified. Heat radiated from his abdomen and raced through his veins. He could smell burning meat but wouldn't – couldn't – admit it had anything to do with him. A whiff of smoke spiralled from his nostrils.

Searing pain ripped through him, forcing a scream from his lips. With the scream came fire. It gushed from his mouth, ensuring that the last thing he saw in this world was the means of his destruction. A moment later, his eyeballs exploded.

Flames erupted from all his pores and orifices. Despite his torment, he did not move. His muscles were turning first to liquid and then to smoke. For a moment that seemed eternal, Donald Haig was deaf, blind and in the grip of an all-consuming agony.

Cernunnos was merciful. With a gesture of his hand, he granted Haig the gift of death. Then he let go of his earthly countenance and flowed back into the skull where he would sleep until he was called upon once more.

Lydia decided she'd seen enough. 'Bag everything up and let's get out of here before the peasants surround the place and try to burn it down.'

'Ma'am?' Sergeant Steele looked at her blankly.

'I think,' said Roger Fleetwood, popping a mint into his mouth, 'Detective Inspector Brooks is inferring that the people of Saighir Village are an ignorant bunch of superstitious yokels.'

'But I'm from Saighir Village. And my folks before me. And my folks before them.'

'Which rather eloquently puts paid to the Inspector's hypothesis. Doesn't it, Inspector?'

'Sure,' said Lydia, thinking that if ever there was a prime example of the sort of hick she had in mind, he was standing right in front of her with three stripes on his arm.

A constable walked in carrying a small, cordless vacuum cleaner. He proffered it to Fleetwood.

'And what,' asked the medical examiner, 'do you expect me to do with that?'

'Dunno, sir. I was told to fetch a vacuum cleaner for you.'

'Do you know how to use it?'

'Of course.'

'Good.' Fleetwood nodded in the direction of the ashes that had once been Donald Haig. 'Try not to leave anything behind.'

Lydia enjoyed watching the constable's face as he got to grips with what was being asked of him. A hint of a grin suggested he thought he was having a joke played on him, but the grin quickly vanished to be replaced by a look of near-panic. He turned to Lydia in the hope that she would spare him.

'When you've done that,' she said, putting on her best poker face, 'my car could do with a clean.'

As the constable set about his unpleasant task, Lydia found her gaze being drawn to the skull – specifically to its empty eye sockets. It made her think how she would look - with luck many years hence - when Death had claimed her and her flesh had gone the way of all things. She hoped her end would be more dignified that the late Mr Haig's.

As happens when someone stares at something too long, Lydia's eyes lost their focus. The skull appeared as two dark patches floating in a mist. Everything else around her vanished.

She watched as the patches seemed to melt and trickle onto the table where they coalesced and formed a pool of absolute darkness. Amused by the tricks her eyes were playing on her, she fought an urge to blink and spoil the illusion.

Somebody screamed.

Lydia snapped out of her reverie as the constable dropped the vacuum cleaner and leapt away from the table.

Roger Fleetwood and Sergeant Steele both had a hand over their mouths and were staring at the skull. Or rather they were staring at the tar-like substance that had filled the skull and was pouring onto the table.

MAGIC NIGHT

A♠

written by J. R. Park

illustrated by M McGee

THE RICH GET THEIR KICKS IN SUCH STRANGE WAYS. DIABLO DIAMONDS KEEPS THE RIFF-RAFF OUT WITH IT'S PRICES. A GLASS OF WATER COST £25.

AND EVERY THIRD SATURDAY IS MAGIC NIGHT.

DEBBIE DIDN'T UNDERSTAND WHY SUCH AN EXCLUSIVE VENUE WOULD HAVE SUCH LAME ENTERTAINMENT. BUT SHE WAS HAPPY TO TAKE THE JOB.

SHE'D BEEN PRACTISING ALL WEEK.

AS THE GREAT FANTASTIQUE INTRODUCES THE TRICK, DEBBIE CLIMBS INTO THE BOX.

NOT THAT THE TRICK REALLY NEEDS INTRODUCING; SAWING THE ASSISTANT IN HALF IS AS OLD AS THE HILLS.

DEBBIE SMILES DESPITE THE DISCOMFORT OF THE BOX.

BUT SOMETHING'S WRONG. SHE CAN'T MOVE HER LEGS TO HER CHEST, LIKE IN PRACTICE. THE BOX IS TOO SMALL.

AS THE SAW'S TEETH TEAR INTO HER SKIN SHE BEGINS TO PANIC.

BUT HER SCREAMS GO UNANSWERED.

THE RICH GET THEIR KICKS IN SUCH STRANGE WAYS.

Dot To Dot

Can you complete this fiendishly difficult dot to dot and identify the lurking horror?

The Girl Who Kissed The Dead
by Tracy Fahey

The first man I ever kissed was my grandad. He was dead at the time.

It wasn't my idea; it was my uncle who insisted.

'Go on. You'll always regret it if you don't say goodbye properly.' His hand was strong on the small of my back, insistent. My eyes were pink-streaked from crying, mostly with relief. I suppose he thought I was distraught. All around me I could hear murmurs of insincere praise and condolence.

'He was a good man, God rest him.'

'He was a lovely footballer in his day. I remember watching him play, oh many's the time.'

'Ah, he's in a better place now.'

I hope he isn't. I hope he's in a worse place. Somewhere he can't shout at us. Or lash out at us, mean as a bad-tempered dog.

'Go on.' My uncle nudges me again. I'm fifteen and pure awkward, not knowing how to say no. His breath is thick and warm in my ear. It smells of ham and sour beer. I flick a look about. Everyone's talking. There's no-one to intervene. My grandad lies rigid, glazed in pale yellow. His face is cut into stark frown lines, but someone has tried to move his lips into a smile. It looks forced, ridiculous on his stern face.

'Go on. Kiss him.'

And I do. His forehead is shrunken, hard and marbelled with cold. It's like kissing a skin-covered stone. I wipe my mouth deliberately and walk away.

It is the first time I've ever kissed him. And it's the last.

These days I kiss who I damn well want. I'm mouthy and badass, with the punk makeup, the purple hair, and the ink to prove it. My arms are a colourful tangle of candy skulls, thorned roses, crosses and hearts. I like darkwave music, the art of Laurie Lipton, loud rock bars and second-hand bookshops. I work in what we euphemistically call the 'end of life' business, softening the ugliness of reality for the grieving. I'm the Mortician Beautician and my business, Dead Beautiful, has been transforming the dead for the last six years. It's popular. I even have a waiting list. But I have my favourites, and my favourite large client is Garvey's funeral home. They have a resident beautician, but they call me in whenever they get a difficult or specific request. Like today.

I stare down at the table in the back room. It smells of chemicals and cold walls.

'So what exactly have they asked for?'

'For her to look happy. To look as fresh and natural as possible. To really capture the lively girl she was.' He pauses and passes the letter to me, as if I need to read it myself.

'There's photographs of her too. Right here.' He clears his throat. Kids are hard for David.

Glossy laughing faces shine out of the photographs; here she's wearing a Frozen outfit, there she's astride a new bicycle, and there she's sporting a missing front tooth. The images are crisp and detailed, and they've provided her favourite clothes. I thrive on challenges, but this one's easy. I nod at him.

'I can do it.'

'Great! I'll leave you to it, so. Don't want to get in the way.' The relief is so palpable in his voice I can hear a slight gasp. 'Cup of tea first?'

'Always.' I rotate my shoulder muscles till they click. The chill in here always makes them ache. When David comes back with a steaming cup – he makes it nice and strong, just how I like it - I'm already at work, cleaning her small face as carefully as possible.

'Another excellent job.'

I smile, pleased, as I wipe down the surfaces. David's father is normally hard to please.

'Nearly done.'

He examines the face carefully, feature by feature. 'It's perfect,' he pronounces. 'Flawless finish. Nice touch of pink there on the cheeks and nose. Lip colour looks lovely and natural.'

'She's a sweet kid. It was a nice job to do.' I hand back the folder with the photos. 'I'll finish up now.'

As the door closes behind, I do the final touches before I pack my equipment away. Slight rumple of the hair. Extra highlighter under the left eye to counteract the darkness underneath. And last of all, a kiss goodbye. I touch my lips to her smooth, cold forehead.

'Goodbye and good luck.'

I love the pleasant dead. They deserve the best. I'll work for hours on their faces, slowly circling contours, building up layers of washed colour to animate their discoloured skin. I'll analyse their photos to find out their favourite looks and colours. I'll brush their hair, as careful and loving as a mother. I'll get lost in time, dotting faces with precise, minute amounts of blush to simulate living, healthy skin. I'll work late, till my arms are stippled with coloured gooseflesh and my nose is sore and damp with cold. I'll work till they look their very best. I'll work and work, and then send them on their way with a kiss for luck.

Like I say, I love the pleasant dead.

My grandfather was far from pleasant. He was a cold, angry tyrant.

At the wake, of course, there's no mention of this. The place is thick with talk, a solid buzz of people coming and going. My granny's soft face is pink and rough from crying, a damp tissue balled in her wrinkled hand. I stand about, tall and awkward, sweating in my black dress. Aunts pass me endless heavy white plates of sandwiches. I heave them onto the crook of my arm and walk around slowly, pausing beside the little groups to offer them up, silently. People slide the sandwiches off the plate, continuing to talk as they do so, continuing to talk even through the visible paste of half-chewed meat and bread as they eat.

'Ah, I remember rightly the last time I saw him. Outside Mass last March. He was very spry then.'

'He had a lovely voice. Didn't sing much these days, but when he was a boy it was lovely.'

'He was sick for a long time, wasn't he?'

I continue to thread my way through the warm crowd. It smells of wet coats and beer and smoke. A woman stops me for a sandwich, saying to her neighbour - 'God bless them all, it's a release.'

'Goddamn right it is!' I snap my head around. It's my cousin Steve, sitting in the corner with a tumbler of whiskey. I haven't seen him in a few years. He's twenty, unemployed the last I heard, tainted with fascinating rumours of bad company and worse deeds. I look him over shyly. He looks out of place in this setting, his face locked in a sneer, his hair greased back, his leather jacket oily and worn. He flicks a sardonic look my way.

'Isn't it? A release?'

'Yeah.' I make sure no-one's listening. 'He was a right old bastard.'

I love my job. I get to do things the nine-to-five crew can't do. Like go to the cinema in the afternoon, or sit in playing games online. When I get bored, or very broke, I moonlight in the tattoo bar. I got into tattooing through my own experiences in being a living canvas; it turns you into a critic and an expert faster than any certified course. My art school training stood to me when I took it up. Drawing on skin is no different to drawing on paper, same skillset, just different surfaces. Now I've trained, I specialise in intricate funereal motifs, and have a small but devoted roster of clients. But if I want a quicker cash injection I'll do a few shifts in Vintage Viv's hairdressing and beauty salon downtown. This afternoon happens to be one of those times. I don't mind. I like going to Viv's. Most of the clientele look like 1940s pinups and – they don't say it, but I know it – they get a kick out of a mortician beautician doing their hair and makeup.

'I'm thinking kinda Amy Winehouse with the hair, but more, I don't know, Gaga maybe with the makeup? It's a roller derby ball so I want to look different.'

The girl in the chair scowls at herself in the mirror, crumpling up her pretty, even features into a snarl. The only way to look really different at a roller derby ball would be to go decked out in complete Laura Ashley, to be honest, but I just nod and look thoughtful. It's already five o'clock and the room smells like hot hair. So far, I've finished working up one faux-Magenta, en route to a Rocky Horror Night, and two girls on their way to a 1940s-style tea-party. This Gaga girl will be my last. I stand behind her and lift her hair, weighing it like a soft cloud in my hands.

'I love your tattoos.'

Great, a talker. 'Uh-huh.' I twist her hair around, experimentally.

'I've been thinking of getting one myself. I've heard it's a good thing to do to mark a big change. And it's been a real year of it.'

She's watching me in the mirror. I nod.

'And for the moment, I just feel like, you know, doing something different with myself. Changing my look.'

I separate and pin her hair into thick strands, and start to painstakingly tease and backcomb them into a bouffant beehive. She keeps talking. I'm used to it. It's the soothing, confessional effect of being in a chair with someone stroking your head. Happens all the time.

'It's been a really crappy time, but I hope it's over now. I finished up with my ex – a complete dog.' Everyone told me he was, of course, but I wouldn't listen, I kept telling them – telling myself – he would get better. He was so lovely when we got together first.' Her voice goes quiet. 'No-one would believe how nice he was to me. He'd go out at three in the morning to get me ice-cream, or stay on the phone for hours. But then we moved in together and then he just changed.'

I know he did. I've separated her hair out and I've seen the scars on her head. She feels my fingers trace over her scalp and her eyes meet mine in the mirror.

'Yes,' she says flatly. 'He did that. And now he's dead and I'm not sorry.'

I tilt her head to one side with my hands and squint at the inky mass of her hair. Her neck looks fragile, bowed under its weight.

'Tell me more.' And she does. It's the usual sad story, but one that never gets any easier to tell. Or hear. It's a tale of sudden tempers. Locking her into the house. Beatings. Hospitalisation. And finally, his death. An OD last week.

'There had to be an autopsy, so it was delayed, the funeral I mean.' It's standard practice in Ireland to plant someone in the ground pretty much as soon as they're dead. The only exceptions are complicated deaths or bodies who need to be repatriated to the UK. I listen as I work, and then spray her huge hairdo hard as steel with my trusty rock-hold hairspray. I can't start on her Gaga makeup yet, tears keep shivering down her cheeks, so I give up for the moment and sit down beside her.

'But I'm going out tonight. That's a start, isn't it? And after his funeral I'll get that tattoo. I will.' Her face is pale and defiant.

'Good for you.' I need to make a call.

At the back of Viv's, I pull my phone, still warm from my leather trouser pocket. I light up a cigarette and suck in deeply. It might take a few calls. I'll try the biggest ones first. Save time. I exhale – a noisy whooooooooo – and start thumb-flicking through my phone address book.

When I get back ten minutes later she's still sitting in exactly the same position.

'Sorry about that'. I'm not though. I'm pretty happy with myself. 'Right. Gaga make-up it is. Tell me what exactly you're thinking of.'

When we're finished - and it's a good job, if I say so myself; she looks like a David Bowie/Three Degrees mashup - I pull her chair backward so she can admire the finished creation.

'That's exactly what I wanted. To look completely different.' She draws in a silent, quivering breath. 'Thank you.' Her eyes sparkle with sudden tears.

'Careful. Don't undo my good work.'

'I'm not going to cry!' She tips her chin out. I like her defiance.

'I might take a photo of you for the salon if that's OK? We always like to photograph the best ones.' I lean over her chair and smile.

'Sure.' She's delighted, strikes a few poses, blowing a kiss, pouting.

I put the camera down and grin back at her. 'Great stuff. I owe you. Meet you across the road at six? I'll get you a drink to say thanks.'

She nods perkily. 'Sure, that'd be great. I'm Holly.'

I grip her hand in a strong handshake. 'I'm Lilith. Lil.'

My granndad was an old bastard, alright. My mum died when I was little so I went to live with him and my granny. It all happened before I was old enough to remember anything else, though sometimes I fancy I recall her through fugitive hints, my mum, that is - a whiff of perfume and the glimpse of a window with flowers oustide. Granny was lovely, all papery-soft skin and warm smells of talc when she cuddled me. She bought me books and made me elaborate dresses, paddling the treadle on the sewing machine with a heavy foot, lips pursed, concentrtaing. I watched her work, lit in the glow of the stove, filled with a scalding tenderness. She loved me and I loved her.

But him. A completely different story. He was a drinker for a start. That was good in the daytime because it meant he wouldn't be home. You could even forget about him for the evening. He'd be in the pub at that stage, stoking a cold fire, raking at the embers till they'd catch fire and blaze. But as soon as it got properly dark everything changed. The house would be quiet, waiting, every sound magnified, every footstep a threat, every voice a danger. Sometimes the waiting was worse than the arrival. But usually it was the arrival that was the worst. It always happened the same way, hard, clunking, overly-deliberate steps crunching on the gravel path. The sequence of sounds is sharp in my memory. The scrabbles of a key against, then near, and then finally in the lock itself. The cursing as he struggled with the handle, the brutal swing and clang of the door against the wall as he stumbled in. If we were lucky he might just come in and shout for a bit before collapsing like a wet paper bag. If we were really lucky he mightn't make it out of the hall. But more often than not we were unlucky. He'd call for my granny, cursing and shouting, and she'd push me upstairs, where I'd hide, hoping to be forgotten. That's my most vivid memory - shut away in the wardrobe upstairs, my own breathing hard in my ears, listening to the shouts, the wet noises of pleading, the dull thumps and thuds as he beat his way upstairs. He beat her soft skin till she was stiff with bruises. Over and over. Everyone knew. He didn't care about it, he was reckless. There was black eyes. Broken wrists. Even once, a palm-print, red as a brand on her cheek. It only stopped when he got sick, sick enough to just lie in bed, yellow and clenched and mean, beating nothing but the floor beneath him with his stick.

And now he's dead and no-one will tell the truth. He's being praised and celebrated. My granny accepts their condolences with a sad, downturned mouth. The talk is hushed and reverent, apart from the rowdy group around the table who are telling tales about him that makes them burst into rough laughter. I can't imagine what these stories are, or what can make them laugh like that. I clench my fingers white-tight around the plates and snap my teeth together in frustration.

I want to tell the truth. I want them all to know.

'You want me to help you in work?' Her face is creased in surprise. I don't know what she expected, but it wasn't this. Maybe she thought it was a date? That's happened before – sometimes people see the tattoos and the piercings and assume I'm fiercely butch.

'Uh-huh.' I take a long swallow of my beer.

'Help you with a body?'

I'm starting to have second thoughts. Maybe I've misjudged her. 'Yes.'

'But I've no experience – I wouldn't know what to do -'

I cut her off with one raised hand. 'Look, if you don't want to, that's fine. I thought it might distract you a bit.' I play my ace. 'I thought you'd be cool. Up for it.'

'Well, yes, sure I am.'

Yup. No-one can ever resist that one. I finish my drink and get up.

'I'll call you tomorrow. And have fun tonight. You look killer.' I point at her, pistol style and aim an imaginary shot at her heart.

It's taken a few hours of careful washing and preparation to undo most of the damage death has caused. I've covered up the skin with my heaviest makeup; thick as Polyfilla, spread like butter onto the face. I stand back and survey it. Open coffin. Never a great idea at the best of times, definitely not when the corpse looks like this. I try to soften the harsh lines of the mouth, but the skin is stony, resistant. I think of my granddad's hideous waxy face and scowl, head to one side. Better than that, at any rate. I wash my hands and start to whistle. The sound rings so nicely against the hard walls that I've whistled Lovecats and almost all of Boys Don't Cry by the time David calls back in to check on my progress.

'Busy for another while?'

I nod. I'm nearly finished, truth be told, but I'm waiting for Holly. Without looking up, I know he's hovering beside me. He's always around, at my elbow, sneaking a look at my tattoos. He does it every time I roll my sleeves up. I get the feeling he's always on the verge of a confession – I know he hates his job though he's never come out and said it. Poor, conventional David trapped with the dead, coffins, and tattooed beauticians. He looks like he dreams of running away to be an accountant.

I don't really think she'll show up, but she does, just when I'm finished prepping the cadaver. David starts when the doorbell goes.

'I think that's for me.' I'm casual, like I always have visitors at the mortuary. He looks puzzled, but goes and answers the door anyway. I go out and meet them in the hall. She looks a lot younger without all the makeup. Her hair is screwed into a tight ponytail that lifts her eyebrows like commas on her forehead.

'David, this is Holly. She's my assistant.'

He looks curious. 'She's on work experience from college, aren't you, Hol? Going to give her a crash course with Dead Beautiful.'

'I'm not sure...' David is hesitating, standing in the doorway of the cold room. The best way to deal with David is to keep talking at him, fluently and persuasively. He's easily convinced.

'Holly, this is David. One of the best morticians I've worked with.' (He isn't.) 'He'll give you the inside scoop. Even a tour if you're lucky. Won't you David?' The compliment and the repetition of his name have made him flush a rosy pink. I feel a little bad. I like David. But this is more important.

'Sure,' he says, smiling at Holly. She smiles back – aha! I think, this might turn out to be a very satisfactory night.

'Shall we?' And they're gone. I go back into the cold room and do a final, meticulous check on the cadaver. Face as good as it can be, hair carefully combed, suit pressed, hands crossed. It'll do. I cover it back up with a clean white sheet, and sit down peacefully, ankles crossed, till I hear a jumble of voices in the doorway.

'It's so interesting!' says Holly, smiling up at David. He is flustered and obviously, comically, flattered.

'Great.' I don't want him lingering. 'David, thanks so much for that. Time for us to get to work now.'

'Sure.' He bobs his head. 'Tea? Both of you?'

'That'd be great.' I wait until till the door closes, one beat, two beats, three.

'Holly?'

'Yes?'

'Deep breaths. I need you to be calm. Very calm.' Her hand flutters to her mouth, her eyes alarmed. I pause, raising a warning finger. 'Deep breaths.'

I keep a tight eye on her. She is still as marble, tense, waiting. 'Still breathing?' My voice is soft, measured, calming. She nods. I peel back the sheet and expose the face.

'Ah!' The squeal is completely involuntary, I know, but I grab her arm anyway. 'Quiet!'

Her mouth is open to a comical extent, her head pivots wildly between me and the drawer, eyes huge with panic. 'Shhhhh,' I say, stroking her arm. 'Shhhh.'

'But!' Her face is full of a dreadful surmise. 'Did you know? Why did you?'

'Yeah. Course I did.' Her mouth opens, incredulous, but I raise a finger again. Careful footsteps in the corridor. It's David coming back. Wait till he goes I mouth at her, and she must have understood because she sucks in a breath so deep I see her nostrils flutter. David's at the door, angling his hip to push it open, attention fixed on the brimming mugs.

'Thanks,' I say, deftly taking them from his hands.

'You OK for everything?' he asks. I nod and smile, and he smiles back, before finally turning and leaving. The door shuts tight behind him with an audible click.

I wait, looking steadily at her. 'OK.' I say finally. 'I knew alright. I knew it was him - I made sure of it in fact. That's why you're here, because it's important.'

She looks at me, her face soft and blind with fear, but she doesn't move. Good.

'Now we've got work to do.'

And that's when I open my other bag.

That night at the wake was a night of firsts. It was the first time I told the truth about my grandad. The first time I was listened to. The first time I took a drink. When I called my granddad a bastard, it made Steve laugh, a big, surprised belly-laugh.

'And you're a right one,' he says approvingly. 'Come and join me for a whiskey.'

'I don't drink,' I say primly.

'You do now.' He pushes a tumbler towards me. I lift it in my hand. It's cool and heavy, the cut glass sparkling in shards of light. His smile is wicked, a challenge. That's how it all starts. I drink the whiskey. It burns a snail trail of luminosity down my throat. I feel magical. Invulnerable. I forget about everything, the plate of hardening sandwiches on the table, my sweaty black dress, even the feel of that frigid, plastinated skin under my lips. I look around a few times for my granny, but she's too busy telling lies and looking sad to notice me. And when Steve gets bored and asks me if I wanted to come into town with him on the back of his motorbike, I say yes.

I go out, get drunk in a bar and get my first tattoo. Steve's friend doesn't care how old I am. I still have it, you know. A neat little headstone engraved with 'Rot In Peace'.

When I get it, it hurts.

And I like it.

It takes a while to calm Holly down, and still more time to convince her about what I'm doing. She's in a state of shock, but I've done this before. I talk to her like I'd talk to a frightened dog, soft and gentle, reassuring. And she's made of stronger stuff than she looks.

She doesn't say anything as I finish dusting the face with powder. At first she just watches, mouth working like she's trying not to scream. But the rhythm soothes her, my practiced hands moving in a complicated dance over the table, my calmness. And she comes closer, closer. Her lips stop chewing over each other. She doesn't protest as I unbutton the shirt and take it off.

'I need to turn him over,' I say, briefly, and she helps me pull and strain till we tumble him over, heavy as a coal-sack. At one stage she even holds down the body while I work. After a while, she's so interested she forgets to be afraid. She asks questions. I even let her take over at one point. (I'm briefly worried about her hands, but they're quite steady). When we finish, even before we take off our gloves, I throw an arm around her shoulders and give her a rough squeeze. It's a job well done. I'm proud of her and she knows it. She hugs me right back, a quick, fierce hug of complicity, body hard against mine.

'We're finished now.' I say. 'Want to step back and take a look?'

She does. We both look. Etched into the discoloured skin of his back is a neat list of what he did to her. The same list she recounted to me in the beauty parlour, tears crawling down her face.

We stand there reading it. I'm admiring my handiwork. I don't know what Holly's thinking till she says in a low voice, 'Thank you.'

'A pleasure,' I say. And I mean it. We stand together in silence. And it's an odd word to use, but we're happy.

This is a strange world we live in, full of our strange rituals. The dead never really stay dead, you know. They stay living; we make them live again. We resurrect them through our funeral rites. We breathe life into them through compliments and stories. We soften their harshness and turn their cruelties into whimsical stories. Even I collude in it. It's my job after all. I paint their faces. I arrange their hair. I make them pretty. I kiss the pleasant dead and send them on their way.

But I don't lie. Not when it comes to the unpleasant dead. I send them to their maker, unmade, exposed. I map their real stories in ink and blood. I incise the truth on their bodies in careful script. Their ugly truths are written in the flesh, layers deep. In the coffin, beneath the ground, in the demure graveyard, their bodies flower in images and words that contradict the careful lies told overhead.

I kiss all the dead you see.

But some I kiss with my needle.

Sinister Horror Word Search

Can you find the 21 hidden book titles?

E	H	S	P	U	T	E	R	R	O	R	B	Y	T	E	D	P	L	M	Y
R	P	G	V	O	M	S	X	W	L	E	M	A	G	D	A	B	E	H	T
V	F	U	R	H	R	F	S	O	K	M	A	I	N	P	K	H	D	E	L
U	K	I	N	G	C	A	R	R	I	O	N	S	T	E	T	U	N	L	D
E	N	J	O	C	F	E	G	B	A	H	M	U	H	A	W	N	U	L	F
O	D	B	P	O	H	N	J	K	D	B	E	V	E	L	G	N	O	S	T
N	R	O	C	I	F	P	M	A	R	K	E	D	E	H	O	S	R	H	G
A	B	D	R	R	U	I	N	A	P	S	A	N	X	L	Y	E	G	I	W
M	G	N	I	S	P	R	O	C	N	A	R	W	C	T	N	O	R	P	B
H	A	X	U	N	I	B	U	R	N	I	N	G	H	O	U	S	E	F	K
C	R	D	B	K	I	E	A	H	J	H	A	X	A	V	E	L	D	N	U
I	F	L	D	G	O	N	P	E	L	E	T	C	N	U	D	W	N	E	P
L	A	H	D	O	N	T	T	E	T	O	F	B	G	P	K	H	U	Y	O
M	X	U	N	D	G	L	I	O	M	I	C	H	E	O	H	A	T	E	N
I	K	I	N	B	P	U	N	F	F	E	J	X	H	S	D	V	S	H	W
E	M	R	R	O	B	E	S	P	I	E	R	R	E	T	G	S	E	L	A
H	E	L	G	M	O	P	F	E	T	D	A	B	N	A	M	O	R	I	K
N	W	X	F	B	J	I	T	L	W	E	P	R	T	L	O	L	O	N	I
U	F	H	D	E	V	I	L	K	I	C	K	E	R	S	N	B	F	M	N
T	N	O	I	C	I	D	L	A	M	G	A	L	X	B	L	J	M	O	G

You mortals occassionally come up with a good idea. Take Lego for example, a child's toy that even makes us dwellers of the dark realms momentarily reduce our hatred and loathing by a fraction. But the one thing you've all got wrong is how nicey-nicey it is. Imagine, just for fun, if Lego made Sinister Horror Sets. What would they look like...

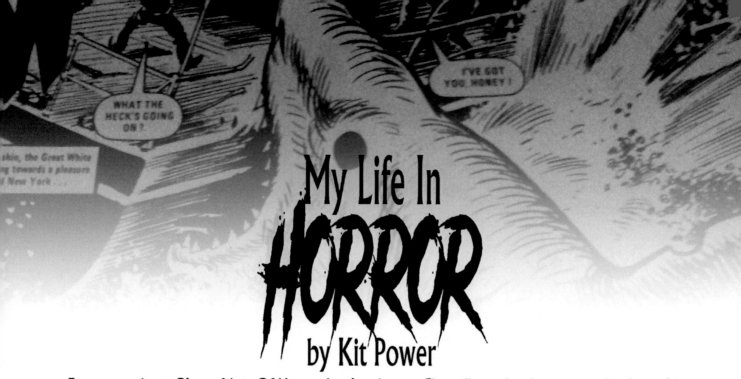

My Life In
HORROR
by Kit Power

Every month, at Ginger Nuts Of Horror I write about a film, album, book or event that I consider horror, and that had a warping effect on my young mind. You will discover my definition of what constitutes horror is both eclectic and elastic. Don't write in. Also, of necessity, much of this will be bullshit – as in, my best recollection of things that happened anywhere from 15 – 40 years ago. Sometimes I will revisit the source material contemporaneously, further compounding the potential bullshit factor. Finally, intimate familiarity with the text is assumed – to put it bluntly, here be gigantic and comprehensive spoilers. Though in the vast majority of cases, I'd recommend doing yourself a favour and checking out the original material first anyway.

This is not history. This is not journalism. This is not a review.

This is my life in horror.

I'LL MAKE YOU BLEED, LIKE I DID

It's January 1989. I am, regular readers will rejoice to hear, eleven years old.

It's January, I know, because it's the January sales, and I am in Exeter city centre, Christmas money from elderly relatives all but burning a hole in my pocket. I am not, as my recollection goes, in the Waterstones where I will later purchase the life changing Death In The Family Batman comic, though that time cannot be far off. I am instead, memory insists, across the other side of the road, in a discount store. And in that store, arranged in sizable stacks on tables near the entrance, are several plies of 1988 Annuals. This being January 1989, these are all heavily discounted - from the £2.99 - £3.75 price point they held in December, when they'd serve as stocking fillers for every unimaginative person with a child in their life, down to an utterly irresistible 99p.

I was a big fan of the Annual back in the day. I'd usually get both Dandy and Beano collections from one family member or another for Christmas, and rare was the 'bring and buy' sale in the village where I didn't come back with an old Spiderman, Daredevil or Superman collection tucked under my arm, complete with felt pen glasses drawn on some of the faces courtesy of the previous owners. You'll be shocked to learn that I still have some of them now, and am contemplating a loft run soon to locate them and figure out which might be suitable for my suddenly-superhero-obsessed eight year old daughter.

They were really cool, those old superhero Annuals. Getting hold of US comics in general was, for a UK eleven year old in North Devon, functionally impossible. The Annuals really were a cultural lifeline - and because of the prestige of the format, they tended to carry the very best stories from the recent comics of the heroes in question - like, one of the Spiderman books has The Night Gwen Stacy Died, and the Daredevil features a superb Black Panther team up. Hell, even the Superman comic featured Supergirl, The Martian Manhunter, and... hmm, either The Spectre or The Phantom Stranger, in a story that ran across the entire book in three parts.

All that's based on pre-loft run recall. Good times, is what I'm trying to say, memorable times.

And then there's Big Adventure Book. The book 11 year old me picked up in that discount store in the strange and distant land of January, 1989.

Looking at the front cover now, it's obvious to me why I gravitated towards it. I'd seen Jaws by this point in my life, so the huge image of Hook Jaw, Deadly Menace Of The Deep was probably enough to prize the pound coin from my sweaty fist, even if it hadn't been accompanied by Dredger, The Ruthless Secret Agent, and the promise of Electrifying Thrills With The Steel Claw.

I had no idea that this was a collection of reprints from the mid-seventies - and how could I, really? - or that the '224 action-packed pages!' would be in black and white. Nor did I have the slightest inkling until much later about the controversy that swirled around the titles these tales first appeared in - Valiant, Vulcan, and of course the tabloid-infamous Action Comic.

The reprint angle I soon figured out. It was obvious from the way the stories were presented - a new title page every 2 - 5 pages, with a succinct summary of the story so far appearing as explanatory text - and it was a format that was familiar to me from my limited exposure to 2000AD. But the 70's-ness of the stories didn't really impress upon me, either then or in a recent re-read. Indeed, until the research I did for this piece, I'd always assumed they were basically contemporary comics, repackaged for the Christmas market.

Part of that is down to the timeless quality of much of the subject matter, I think. Hook Jaw follows a huge man-eating Great White (as this collection opens, he's been hunting in the oceans near the UK, which I can only fondly imagine is a prequel story I have yet to read) who ends up, by a series of unfortunate events, in the Hudson River, NYC, striking a pose with his fin against the background of the Statue Of Liberty and eating tourists.

Similarly, The Lout That Ruled The Rovers and Wizz Along Wheeler feature respectively Division Four football grounds and a circus featuring a wall of death motorcyclist with dreams of winning The Big Race, neither of which settings scream 70's to a child of the 80's. Add in the evergreen setting of Nazi-occupied France in The Black Crow, and rural Wales under threat of alien invasion in The Steel Claw, and I think the oversight is understandable. Sure, One Eye Jack and Dredger (New York Cop/ DI6 secret agent fight terrorism/espionage in NYC/London) might have given the game away, especially with their haircuts and dress sense, but on the other hand, fighting the commies was as hot for most of the 80's as it was the 70's. So sure, once you know that, there are joys to be found; especially in comparing the latter two characters to their barely-disguised source material of Dirty Harry and The Professionals/The Sweeney-meets-Bond.

But fundamentally, the joy is just in the stories themselves.

I mean, let's just get this out of the way - they're problematic in exactly the ways you'd expect. For starters, they are incredibly, graphically violent. While actual severed limbs are rare, Hook Jaw rarely gets through five pages of strip without eating someone - often many people - and there are several images of people seconds away from death by shark that are, frankly, terrifying and brilliant. Similarly, Dredger shoots, beats, and electrocutes his way through life in a way that leads nothing to the imagination. And, perhaps predictably, The Black Crow is the worst of the lot, featuring not just regular scenes of people getting shot and blown up in battle but scenes of gestapo torture that I still find stomach churning.

And, as you'd expect from fiction produced in the 70's aimed at boys, half the population basically doesn't exist. With the notable exception of Wizz-Along Wheeler, which features a moment of comical surprise as our hero discovers his helmeted bike rival is actually *gasp* female (actual quote: "Well, blow my gasket! I've just been given the race of me life by a perishin' GIRL!"). Women exist, if at all, to either be eaten by sharks, or victimized by Nazis, and... that's it. And part of me feels stupid even bringing it up, because, well, duh, but a bigger part would feel stupider if I didn't, so there it is.

And, you know, the German Nazis are Comic Book Germans to a man, and some of the language, while not top level offensive, is certainly... not how we would phrase things now. The national stereotypes apply across the board, actually, providing an inadvertently hilarious insight into what Brits of a certain age thought were the defining characteristics of various peoples of Europe and America.

Still, though, and for all of that, the stories are still the stories, and they still crackle with a vivid energy. For all it's fair to say that they were not written to be re-read - by which I mean, in addition to the aforementioned recap every few pages thing, there's a certain repetition of story beats and even dialogue in places - there is a pleasure to be had in the sheer pace and spectacle of the thing. I remember as a kid being enraptured by the sheer epic scale of Hook Jaw's odyssey, and the way he flips between roles of antagonist and protagonist. It's still a surprisingly schizophrenic narrative, in that regard - in the opening chapters, Hook Jaw is unambiguously our POV character, and we're invited to sympathize with him in his initial battles with whaling ships, other sharks, and finally a giant fucking squid. Equally, once he arrives at Manhattan island, the POV shifts to the poor humans who end up in the river, and then, in short order, in Hook Jaw's gullet, but our sympathies swing back as he is captured and experimented on (and indeed tortured by a previous attack survivor who now works as a janitor in the shark research facility, thus proving that even in the 70's HR departments were hilariously awful at vetting job applications).

It really, really shouldn't work, and yet it does - despite the hokey characters and stilted dialogue and absurd level of incident. In fact, let's be honest, it's because of the absurd level of incident this story, and indeed all the stories really work. The sheer pace of the next thing happening propels you through worrying about how many ridiculous things have happened in a row, the constant boggling of the mind serving as an insulation against the otherwise inevitable 'wait, what?'

It's nothing bigger or more clever or more complicated than the joy of pulp storytelling. And for all that Big Adventure Book carries all the flaws from that style of storytelling, and the era in which it was created, it remains a joy to read, at least for me. The black and white art is workmanlike, but with the odd flourish of composition that will elevate a page. The constant sense of peril and stakes, underlined by the graphic bodycount, gives an undeniable dirty thrill to proceedings, a sense of danger both textual and metatextual. Rereading it today, I can see it's fingerprints all over my work, especially that aesthetic of relentless incident and violent danger that so drove my first novel. More, it reminds how, again and again, I am most drawn to work that recreates that feeling of being dragged through a narrative on meat hooks, surrounded by an exploding landscape and towards an uncertain destination.

The Big Adventure Book was, without doubt, a wildly unsuitable piece of entertainment for an 11 year old boy.

I was very lucky indeed to have it.

KP
25/8/18

STRANGER

Written by J. R. Park

I'VE BEEN SAT HERE FOR A WHILE.

WAITING FOR MY FRIENDS.

I DON'T KNOW WHO OR WHAT IT IS, BUT IT'S BEEN WATCHING ME FOR A WHILE.

STARING.

IT'S GIVING ME THE CREEPS BUT I CAN'T STOP LOOKING. IS THIS EVEN REAL?

IT FEELS LIKE A DREAM.

AT FIRST THEY MEAN NOTHING TO ME, BUT THE LONGER I STARE THE MORE FAMILIAR THE FRAGMENTS BECOME.

I SEE A MYRIAD OF FACES; FRAGMENTS ALL FADING IN AND OUT OF VIEW, WARPING AND BLEEDING INTO EACH OTHER.

UNCLE STEPHEN, PETER, BECCA, MY DAD.

BUT I CAN'T LOOK AWAY.

I CAN'T STOP STARING.

MY STOMACH CHURNS. MY HEAD POUNDS. BUT MY GAZE CAN NOT BE BROKEN.

AS THE FACES APPEAR I FEEL THEIR LIVES. THEIR MINDS BEGIN TO FILL MY THOUGHTS.

THE GALLERY OF EXPRESSIONS BEGIN TO MELT. AND I'M EVEN MORE HORRIFIED WHEN ONLY ONE FACE REMAINS.

MY OWN.

I'VE BEEN SAT HERE FOR A WHILE.

I DON'T KNOW WHO OR WHAT IT IS, BUT IT'S BEEN WATCHING ME FOR A WHILE.

WAITING FOR MY FRIENDS.

STARING.

IT'S GIVING ME THE CREEPS BUT I CAN'T STOP LOOKING. IS THIS EVEN REAL?

IT FEELS LIKE A DREAM.

White Knuckle Ride
by Tim Clayton

You want a horror story? I can't really give you one. I don't do horror. The only horror film I've seen as an adult was when the curator of this very annual dragged me to an underground cinema with cold-sweating stone walls to watch a re-release of The Exorcist. My 12-step sponsor says that, at forty years of age, I need to finally start acting like an adult and get over this irrational fear. He suggests that I watch a triple bill of Nightmare on Elm Street, Candyman and Pet Cemetery. This is a very specific and considered suggestion. It is the same triple bill that my older sister made me watch on pirated VHS tapes, when she locked me in a room at the age of six. I doubt she knew at the time that 34 years later I would still be scarred by it.

I can't write a real horror story because I don't read or watch real horror stories. So, here is what a horror story is to me...

I have what may be termed "compulsive curiosity". This means that I generally feel duty-bound to try anything I hear about. I have to squeeze the essence out of everything that life has to offer. This is a wonderful way to become a man of the world. It opens me up to new experiences—like snorkeling in Australia or waltzing along a Brazilian street at midnight. Compulsive curiosity can be a beautiful thing; it talks to that part of the human spirit that says you should try everything once. However, it's also the aspect of my own character that led me to snorting vodka up my nose from a spoon, smoking heroin, and getting into a bunch of trouble over a very long stretch of years before I finally settled down.

I may have put the brakes on but I still get those same impulses. It doesn't matter if it is a good idea or a bad idea, the compulsion to try new things is often all-consuming and overwhelming until it is satisfied.

A few years ago I read a book about the 1996 Everest disaster. Eight people died in a blizzard that lasted for two days in May. Two days of sub-zero temperatures, whiteouts, confusion, and death. Those that did survive had to have their hands, noses or feet amputated due to severe frostbite. And they were the lucky ones. Reading the book, all I could think about was how pathologically obsessed these people were. I felt sorry for them and for their families. And yet, a month later, in mid-January, I organized a trip to the top of the highest mountain in Poland, in temperatures of minus 15 Celsius, because I couldn't get the Everest story out of my mind until I had lived it—or at least as close as I could come to it without spending $50,000.

The moth to the flame. Over and again.

Good and bad in equal measure. It propels me through life and it leads me to trouble.

Now and again, I hear a story that stops me in my tracks. A few months ago I was reading the newspaper and there was a report about a devoted father who just snapped. He was driving on a main road; a typical dual-carriageway on a quiet night. A truck was coming the other way. He calmly called to his kids in the back seat and told them to unbuckle their seatbelts for a moment. And then he swerved.

There was a picture with the article. A mangled mess of metal. No flesh—that had been redacted from the image—but the editor still couldn't resist showing as much of the carnage as decency would allow. Just enough for people to look at the article and say "How could he?" and then go about their days.

Oh, boy. How could he?

I'm not suicidal. I'm in a happy marriage. I love my kids to death.

How could he do it?

I read the article, went to work, and thought nothing about it until the early evening. I'm a father of four. That night I had a typical twenty-minute drive out of town to some bullshit training session or other, where the older kids half-heartedly engage while I stand freezing on the sidelines with the baby. I then praise their effort while feeling inwardly resentful that it cost me a half a day's wages and three hours of my life.

I got the baby in the front seat, buckled the three older ones in the back of the car, and then started the drive. It was dusk. An easy run once rush hour was finished—not that it ever really seems to finish nowadays.

I pulled out of the car park and the kids started asking me about something or other. If you don't have children, or if you have just one, you'll get a common piece of advice from people. Their conventional wisdom goes like this: 'Make sure you have kids that are close together in age; then they will play with one another.' Don't believe it. It's a lie. The loner kids will sit in their rooms all the time. The mixer kids will find friends who are not their siblings. And the kids who lack the confidence to be alone will turn to their parents for validation—they will falsify conversations they think will interest you and bombard you with questions just to keep you close.

We pull off down the road; there is a little spitting mizzle coming down outside. It's the kind of weather where it is difficult to know if the wipers will clear the rain or if they will smear the windscreen and make it even harder to see.

Meanwhile, inside the car the people-pleasing questions are raining down from that one kid that can't go without the attention: Do I want my football team to win this weekend? How was my day at work? Did I enjoy my dinner? What's my favorite place to go on holiday? It takes up half of my brain to process the answers and I'm losing track because they come faster than I can keep up. The other half of my brain power is focusing on the drizzle that is now turning into real rain, the glare from street lights, and the creeping suspicion that I've missed my turning.

That means there is none of my mind left to really notice the truck coming from the opposite direction and appreciate that I have edged the car slightly closer to the centre of the carriageway. It has happened subconsciously. Just a moth to a flame. It's only when I catch it—seconds before the truck thunders past—that I am able to move the car back a few inches from the central line to the safer part of the road.

Just a few inches. And yet it actually takes all of my strength to force the wheel that fraction of a turn that will make the car drift back to where we should be. And there is a fraction of a second where the urge to flick the car across the road into the oncoming truck is almost overwhelming. Moving the wheel that way is no effort at all; moving it away from danger is like turning a capstan in the driving rain.

I look at the tail lights of the lorry in my wing mirror. Only I know what just happened. The fractions of inches would not have been enough for a truck driver to even notice as he carved on into the night.

The lights on the carriageway shine in through the windscreen. I look down at my knuckles and they are white from where I have been gripping the wheel so tightly. The baby is asleep in her chair on the passenger seat. The kids in the back are still talking, or fighting, or singing. But I can't hear them anymore. I'm deaf. I'm drowning in a storm. I am paralyzed and being covered in dirt. The only things I see are a stream of white lights coming towards me on the other carriageway and my own white hands.

How could he do it?

I love my wife and kids. I actually don't even mind myself most of the time. I tolerate my own bullshit well enough to not want to kill myself. And yet, I know that for the rest of my life, every single time I drive that car, curiosity might finally just get the better of me if I lose concentration for a single moment—even for a fraction of a second. Every tiny, unmeasurable moment of unguardedness is a potential enemy.

And they would ask: 'How could he do it?' and they wouldn't know that I didn't do it at all. It was done to me, long ago, before I had the chance to protect myself from the harm.

The Sinister Horror Company take pride in matching the quality content with an equally impressive cover. In order to get the right image, different versions are mocked up and worked through with the artist and author. Over the next few pages we'll show alternative covers that didn't quite make the cut.

Upon Waking

author: J. R. Park
photographer: Thomas Dando
design: Vincent Hunt

The main concept for the cover of Upon Waking by J. R. Park came from the photographer behind the image, Thomas Dando. However it wasn't until Sinister logo designer Vince Hunt got hold of the image, adding a texture like torn skin and creating a degraded title, did it realise its true grindhouse potential.

The cover for Daniel Marc Chant's Burning House was very much a labour of love with both the author and the artist very familiar with the concept and inspiration behind the book. With this being the first release a few layouts were created. The sideways title was dismissed for the more dramatic rush of fire leading upwards to the elegant and startling font.

Burning House

author: Daniel Marc Chant
art and design: Vincent Hunt

Forest Underground

author: Lydian Faust
photographer: Jem Salmon
design: J. R. Park & Vincent Hunt

As always the starting point of this cover was to ask the author what they envisioned. Lydian suggested the image of a tree with a negative polarisation of the image. Justin created a draft using a picture from Jem Salmon, a photographer he had always admired. Not happy with the lack of eye-catching bite to the idea, it was passed to Vince Hunt to alter the image and make it pop.

What Good Girls Do's cover came from a concept sketched out by the author, Jonathan Butcher. Jonathan then organised the photograph that formed the basis of the design. Passed to Vince Hunt, the graphic wizard created a gloriously vibrant cover. Jonathan asked for the colour pallete to be less lurid, with the focus being on the light pouring from the open doorway illuminating the titular girl.

What Good Girls Do

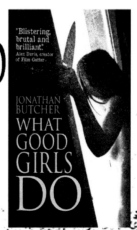

author: Jonathan Butcher
photographer: Sian Jansen-Bowen
design: Vincent Hunt

What if Lego got nasty and made Sinister Horror Sets...

18+

SHC006

Murderous Mermaid

18+

SHC007

The Stygian Confrontation

18+

SHC008

Mitch 'Mad Dog' Mooney

NOT LEGO

SINISTER HORROR COMPANY

18+

SHC009

The Darkling
Shadow
Fight Set

NOT LEGO

SINISTER HORROR COMPANY

18+

SHC010

Rampaging
Unicorn
Set

THE EXCHANGE

J. R. PARK

NOT LEGO

SINISTER HORROR COMPANY

18+

SHC011

Postal
Attack Set

MATT SHAW POSTAL J.R PARK

The Last Patrol
by Andrew Freudenberg

The fat man leant back and drained the whiskey bottle dry. With a groan of satisfaction he licked his lips before pulling himself up and onto his feet.

'Goddamn', he muttered, slamming the empty vessel down onto a pile of boxes masquerading as a makeup table. 'You know', he slurred in a deep voice still redolent of good breeding and an expensive education, 'I saw him without the paint once.'

The boy eyed him warily. 'No, you never did.'

He had lost count of how many times he'd heard this lie.

They looked at each other dolefully. Outside the wind and rain continued to thrash the small tent without mercy. Puddles of water were gathering around the edges of the canvas walls and the air was damp and cold. Somewhere in the distance an angry lion roared

Without warning the entrance flap was flung aside. The newcomer was just over six feet tall and of solid build. A razor sharp crew cut sat atop a chiseled face painted with green and orange stripes. His skin glistened with moisture from the downpour. He glanced around the tent with black eyes more akin to those of an animal than a man, saw no strangers, and then visibly relaxed.

'Boy. Doc.'

The older man nodded in greeting, one corner of his orange lips turning up slightly.

'Good to see you Sarge.'

The youth nodded and shuffled his feet silently.

'It's looking ugly out there.'

Sarge wandered over to the makeshift clothes rail that they had constructed from a couple of pitchforks and a length of rope. He peeled off his khaki t-shirt, revealing a muscled torso patterned with burn scars and a livid pink line stretching from neck to navel. The butt of a Colt Commander protruded from the waistband of his combat trousers. The others watched as he pulled it out and dropped it onto the floor before selecting a bright green satin jumpsuit with fluffy white buttons and cuffs. Outside there was a crash of thunder and the storm stepped up a notch.

The boy cleared his throat.

'I was thinking about the routine...'

Sarge cut him short, his expression grim.

'We don't change the plan. It's worked so far and that's good enough for me.'

He kicked off his mud splattered combat boots and stepped into the suit before shrugging it over his arms.

'Now zip me up.'

Doc watched them for a moment, lost in thought. He turned away and stared into the cracked mirror nestled amongst the discarded tubs of powder and paint. Red eyes and a bloated white face stared back at him. The years hadn't been kind and his reflection disgusted him. With a sigh he turned his attention to straightening his enormous yellow Afro wig.

'Got any of your specials, Doc? I need something to pick me up.'

'Here's your case.'

The boy ran over to scoop it up from a brown pool of muddy water.

Doc settled the battered black bag on his knee and undid the bronze clasp. He peered inside. Where once there would have been order there was now chaos. Brown pill bottles lay strewn amongst surgical instruments that had seen better days. He selected one marked 'Dexamphetamine' that nestled in the grasp of a pair of plasma flecked obstetrical forceps. Sarge took it and popped the lid before upending it into his mouth.

'Has anyone checked the Jeep? I don't want a repeat of last time.'

Sarge shuddered before leaning down to retrieve his boots and pistol.

'I think Jones checked it out,' Doc offered.

'I hope so. We'll use the same formation as we always do. Boy driving and you on spotlight, Doc. I'll take the main gun.'

Doc looked down at his swollen hands, hands that had decided the fate of countless innocents in his previous life. They were trembling.

'Fine. Whatever you say.'

The boy nodded agreement. 'Sure.'

'Good. Now, where the hell is my nose?'

The Jeep had seen better days but Jones, the Circus handyman, did the best that he could with it. A coating of white paint and purple polka dots concealed filled bullet holes surprisingly well. Fur seat covers did an admirable job of keeping the ingrained bloodstains out of sight. A spotlight had been welded on to the machine-gun mounting and a compressed air powered cannon shot confetti from the rear.

The trio ducked into the backstage area, shaking off the rain as they entered. Sarge looked at the jeep, cast in shadow, and sighed. He could still see the cracked paint and torn seats. He could still see the ghosts, still hear their screams and smell their burning flesh.

'OK men, buckle up. It's show time.'

They took their places silently and sat listening as the muffled sounds of the arena washed over them. The boy wiped his hands on his tartan trousers nervously. His teeth chattered in the cold. He hated waiting. He'd spent too many years waiting in vain for someone to rescue him from the clutches of those wretched nuns.

'Start her up...'

In the main arena the music built to a crescendo and came to an end. The crowd roared and out marched half a dozen sweat soaked Chinese knife throwers. Automatically Sarge covered their movements with the cannon. All except one ignored him but their leader stopped for a moment and met his gaze. He was an intimidating individual with a furious stare and tattoos of snarling Dragons that covered both arms. Time flickered for a moment as the two men in silk weighed each other up in the semi-darkness, eyes blazing and lips curled.

'We are go!' screeched the boy, as two emaciated girls in sparkling leotards pulled back the sheets covering the entrance. Sarge drew his finger across his throat before turning away as the engine roared into action.

'Entrance of the Gladiators' blasted out of the PA and the lights dimmed as the boy swung them into an orbit along the arena's periphery. Doc bit his lip and sent the spotlight arcing across the crowd. Fragments of faces and body parts were illuminated momentarily by its glare. His grip tightened around the rubberised handles as he looked out at the multitude, inspecting them for imperfections, evaluating their suitability for surgery. They stared back, unaware of the mental dissection that they were undergoing.

He wondered if they were in Massachusetts; or even worse perhaps they were actually in Boston. He had found that it helped his nerves to be unaware of where the circus was playing. Of course it wasn't always possible to avoid finding out but alcohol and tranquilisers helped him remain unconscious and oblivious much of the time.

Boston. There were a lot of people in that City who would love to get their hands on him. Sometimes he would dream that they had finally caught up with him and that the roles had become reversed. He would see himself strapped to the operating table while they crowded around him, their faces hidden by surgical masks. As they leant down over him with their scalpels at the ready he would try to scream, but the anesthetic wouldn't let him.

It had seemed unfair that he had received so many death threats during the court case. After all, the jury had come to the conclusion that he wasn't responsible for his actions.

Nobody actually knew whom he had deliberately helped to die. It was between him and the Creator and not the domain of lesser mortals. The voices had assured him that he was on the side of good, saving the chosen from future wretchedness and suffering. He'd had the sense not to share that information with anybody, especially not that erroneously self-righteous Judge, and silence had earned him a relatively fortunate verdict.

After serving his spell in the sanatorium he had not gone back. His time spent with the criminally insane could not be described as pleasant but it had been informative. He had learnt that he didn't belong amongst the complacent and comfortable. He told himself that no one knew who he had been, that nobody could possibly recognise him dressed as he was. Still, his mouth was dry as he stared out at the crowd.

Overhead the lighting operator switched everything to green just as two enormous mortars fired shredded silver paper in a plume over the crowd. Sarge blinked, attempting to clear the salt lacing his eyes. For a moment he thought he saw paratroopers descending from overhead but shook off the hallucination and turned his attention to the stalls. A group of youngsters were caught by Doc's spotlight for a split second, their eyes wide with wonderment and a touch of fear.

It was enough to send Sarge back to the jungle, back to the children in the village. Their eyes had been the same, gazing up at him intently, even after he had slaughtered them with his bayonet and laid them all out in a row. At the time it had seemed the kind thing to do, a mercy killing of sorts. After all they had executed everyone else, so who would have looked after them? There was something complete about leaving them lying peacefully amongst the burning buildings. It had been a Zen moment.

The jungle was a rebirth for him. He had been an overgrown boy of twenty-one when the call came. His ambition had been to be a comic actor of all things, something that seemed impossible to imagine now. A seemingly endless stream of auditions had led to nothing and then Uncle Sam had written demanding his help. For a split second he had wondered about hiding in Canada. The notion was probably just a reflection of the liberal attitudes of those around him but he had thought better of it anyway. He kissed his wife goodbye and took the Greyhound across country, as ordered, to Fort Polk. His heart had swelled with pride when they gave him his uniform and when he was handed his M16 he had almost fainted with joy.

After basic training he had shipped out and arrived just as the Tet Offensive was at its peak. When they camouflaged his face at Khe Sanh he knew that this was his destiny. This was the only role that he had been born to play. As they crept through the undergrowth, struggling to breathe in the humidity, he was possessed by the muse. Tearing into those villages, deafened by the clatter of their own guns and the screams of their enemies, he had given the performance of his life.

Up front the boy had flicked a switch, sending a thick cloud of red smoke trailing out behind them. Sarge looked at it grimly before priming the release mechanism on the steel canister down by his feet. The jeep completed its first lap and Sarge opened fire. His eyes narrowed as the rainbow projectiles arced out over the crowd.

Doc was hauling himself up onto his seat, using the spotlight as a lever. Forcing a smile onto his face he let go with one hand and waved at the crowd. The Jeep swerved slightly as they took the corner and he fell onto one knee, hitting his nose on cold steel as he went. Automatically he put his hand to his face and it came away bloody.

'Jesus Christ boy, you'll pay for that.'

In the front seat the boy heard nothing. As always his thoughts were elsewhere, fragile images from his past flashing through his mind. His traitorous mother's face blaming him for his father's death; raised fists raining down on him endlessly throughout his time at the orphanage. He blinked as the slideshow continued. Father O'Brian's oily smile as he towered over him; the filthy hobos who offered him shelter and then used him as a diversion from their own empty existences. In his mind's eye he could still see the razor flashing as it unmanned the Godless Priest and eviscerated those faithless drifters. The tiny blade had been his only friend, the only one who ever stood up for him. He still carried it at all times just in case he needed someone to stand up for him again. His knuckles whitened as he gripped the wheel tighter. His foot pushed a little harder on the accelerator.

Sarge had run out of ammunition. The gun in his boot scratched at his ankle, reminding him that it was there. He ignored it and climbed over into the back seat. Doc grinned at him with crimson stained teeth. He shook his head. Sarge stared at him for a moment before turning away and tapping the boy's shoulder. The two men held on as the Jeep decelerated rapidly before coming to a skidding halt in the sawdust. The lights dimmed and a strobe light started up, slicing their movements into stuttering monochrome.

'Out!'

Sarge hit the ground and rolled into a somersault. Doc stood and managed to trip over the edge of the Jeep, landing heavily on his hands. The crowd roared its approval, taking it to be a part of the act. Sarge ran to him and hauled him upright. For a second they stood there looking out at the crowd before jogging in opposite directions around the vehicle. Doc wheezed and spat the occasional gobbet of blood while Sarge ran slowly and steadily, a thousand yard stare on his face.

The boy leant over and retrieved an old-fashioned bulb horn from the passenger foot well. He then extricated himself from behind the wheel and marched over to the audience barrier, swinging his arms as he went. Even though he measured in at over six feet his head barely reached over the top of the solid wooden wall. So it was that he came face to face with a little girl with blond locks and a dress that should never been seen outside of fairy tales. She stared into his cold blue eyes and found nothing to like. Her bottom lip began to tremble. Adjusting her focus she took in the streaked white face paint and cracked red nose. The tremors spread. For want of anything else to do, the boy unleashed a smile. The sight of his blackened and broken teeth triggered a veritable facial earthquake as she opened her mouth in order to inhale enough oxygen for an ear splitting wail. Before she could start he whipped the horn over the barrier and into her face, unleashing an enormous volley of honking sounds as he did so. He was on his way back to the Jeep before she had even filled her lungs.

Sarge and Doc were still running round in circles but when they saw his approach they stopped and grabbed their ankles. Boy performed a leapfrog manoeuvre over each of them, squeezing the horn victoriously at the apex of each jump. When he had finished, the trio clambered back into the car.

With Boy putting the pedal to the metal they performed another circuit at breakneck speed. A morose silence hung over them as the music faded before segueing into a drum roll. Having completed their final tour they slowed to a halt once more. Sarge turned to face inwards towards the centre of the arena. He raised his hand in a fist and almost magically a circle of flame appeared in the darkness. Next to it a ramp revealed itself in the firelight.

When he'd returned from in country and discovered that his wife had run off with one of the local cops, Sarge had lost himself in the bottle for a week. Then he picked himself up and made it his business to beat the usurper to a bloody lifeless pulp. It had made perfect sense. If he had learned one thing from the Marine Corp it was how justice worked and right was on his side. Of course he couldn't expect civilians to understand. They were sheep and he was the shepherd. They didn't have to make things right in the world; that was his job. He told his shattered wife that he loved her and then ran. As he ran he saw that the sheep didn't appreciate the hell that he had lived through in order to make their lives possible. In fact they positively denounced it. The enemy had won. They had become us and there was no good left in the world anymore.

Sarge leant over and whispered into the boy's ear. 'Do it.'

The engine roared as the boy slammed it down a gear and jammed the wheel round anti-clockwise as far as it would go. The music stopped and the crowd fell silent as they hurtled towards the ramp, isolated in the vehicle from the rest of the world. Sarge's fingers twitched, muscle memory recalling the sweet release of a trigger squeeze. Doc locked his hands together as he remembered what it had been like when he had the power of life and death over others. The boy simply screamed as he pushed pedal to metal.

They hit the ramp too fast and too wide and instantly they knew it was all wrong. The vehicle tilted down to one side as they hit the flaming hoop and by the time it hit the floor they were upside down. The boy was thrown clear and landed in a heap to one side.

The first to emerge from the inverted Jeep was Doc. His wig was gone and he was cradling his right arm with the left. His face was a mask of blood, both from his nose and a fresh gash across his forehead. He looked about, seemingly unsure where he actually was, and stumbled forwards a few feet before stopping. He looked back at the four wheels spinning in the air just as a solitary flame licked out across the exposed underside. Startled he stepped back and immediately fell over the boy and landed on his back. His arms and legs waggled in the air for a few seconds before he managed to roll over onto his hands and knees. He looked at the ragged pile in front of him.

'Boy?' Cautiously he turned the body over. It was immediately obvious from the angle of the head that the boy's neck had been broken. A tear rolled down Doc's face paint. 'Boy?'

The fire had enveloped the Jeep more thoroughly now but miraculously Sarge emerged from the wreckage in a crawl. The front of his jumpsuit had been torn away and his face was covered in cuts. His conical hat had lost the pom pom from the top but was managing to cling on to his head despite its battered state. In a crouch he jogged over to Doc and Boy.

Doc looked up at him. 'I haven't got my bag, Sarge. Have you seen my bag?'

'It's alright, Doc. It's alright.'

From the blackness a group of figures started to emerge. Sarge pulled the Colt from his boot and waved it at them.

'Get the hell back.'

Somewhere up near ringside a woman started crying.

A lone figure stepped forwards from the other would be rescuers. It was the leader of the knife throwing group, his knives now safely tucked into his waistband. He raised his hands over his head.

'We just want to help.'

'I said keep the hell back.'

'We need to put the fire out Sarge. If you...'

'Next one is in your head, now stay back.'

The shot sent the others scurrying back into the shadows but the knife thrower remained. He stood and watched them, his head bowed slightly.

Doc looked up at Sarge. 'Is this the end?'

'We're surrounded. I can't see a way out.'

Doc stared at the boy's lifeless face.

'I don't think I can carry on, Sarge. I'm done. I hate to ask you but do you think...'

'Of course.'

The bullet did its job instantly and Doc's life left him. He slumped down onto the boy's chest. Sarge took aim at his would be rescuer.

'This has been a long time coming...'

The fuel tank exploded, swiftly followed by the compressed air canister. With a deafening boom a ball of flame expanded outwards and upwards, engulfing and evaporating the trio instantly. When the inferno finally subsided all that remained were unclaimed memories and the sound of one man clapping.

CRASh

WE'D NEVER GATE CRASHED A MASQUERADE BEFORE.

LISBETH HAD STOLEN TWO FINE GOWNS.

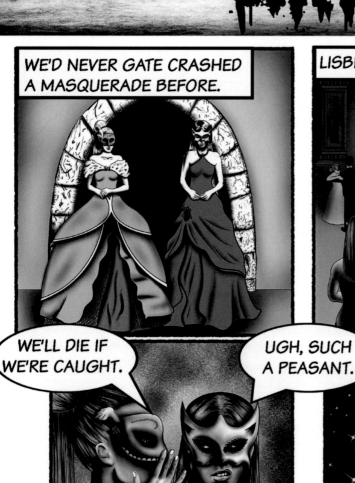

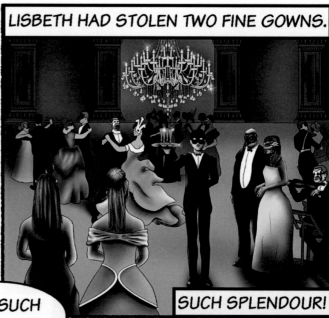

SUCH SPLENDOUR!

WE'LL DIE IF WE'RE CAUGHT.

UGH, SUCH A PEASANT.

FORGETTING OUR FEARS, LISBETH GOT WASTED.

AND WE DANCED OUR SLIPPERS THREADBARE.

BEFORE WE KNEW IT THE CLOCK STRUCK TWELVE.

written by Lydian Faust   illustrated by Jorge Wiles

Naked Wings
by Mark Cassell

Another crow slid through the milky embrace of moonlight and crashed into the field. Many black bodies writhed in the ploughed earth. Their caws echoed, bouncing off the farmhouse, off the barns and the stables, and from the trees. Shrill and ringing.

Stephen squinted through the foliage. His hands pressed into the soil, and dew soaked his pyjamas. Mom and Dad were still watching TV so most likely couldn't hear those crows. That noise had yanked him from sleep and curiosity sent him tiptoeing from the house. He'd be grounded for a week if caught.

More zigzagged from above, tumbling. They landed with a thump and a plume of dirt; dark lumps in the churned soil cawing ever-louder. Some laid sideways, others on their backs, all kicking tiny legs. Loose feathers puffed up, floating.

And more crows crashed down.

So much noise.

Every crow seemed to be suffering a seizure. Stephen had no idea what could cause this. Perhaps they had some disease, the poor things. He leaned forward, pushing his head through tangled branches. One whipped his face and he held it aside.

In a blur of dirt and flapping wings, their bodies throbbed as if expanding. Difficult to see beneath strained moonlight, but to Stephen it appeared as though each crow grew like an inflating beach ball. Those claws jerked, and still they cawed ... cried. More feathers filled the air and lazily drifted away. Legs fattened, extended and thrashed.

The cries intensified into screams.

Stephen cupped his ears, and his heartbeat pulsed in his head. His breath snatched as he failed to understand.

Feathers fell away and the bodies became pale, bloated things. They squirmed. Naked wings scratched in the dirt. Raw skin glistened and stretched, wrinkled. Now completely featherless. Legs kicked ... and was that an arm, like a baby's puffy limb?

Tiny hands with splayed fingers clutched for the moon.

Cigarette smoke drifted on the breeze: Dad.

Stephen's heart punched his ribcage and he fell back into the bushes. His hands slapped the ground, and sticks and stones raked his flesh. The screams tore through him as he watched mouths gape, the noise shrieking from tiny throats. Barely any louder than these screaming crows – babies, they were all now babies – Dad's voice crept toward him:

'Put me through to the maternity department.'

More smoke drifted, more screams echoed.

'Hi, yes, we've had a delivery.'

Stephen held his breath.

'Several dozen,' Dad continued, 'but we'd like to keep one ... No, it would be our second ... Nine years ago ...'

The moon hid behind the clouds.

'... We called it Stephen.'

SINISTER HORROR CARDS

Punch vs The Chocolateman.
King Carrion vs The Death's Head Program.
Who will win?

Now you can find out as you battle with your favourite Sinister
Horror monsters in the Sinister Horror Card game.

Containing 32 individual battle cards and advanced rules for additional gaming.
Available via SinisterHorrorCompany.com

Create your own Sinister Horror Card.

Create a card of your own design to battle alongside all your favourite Sinister monsters in the Sinister Horror Card game.

Add the name of your monster here.

Add a picture of your monster here.

If your monster comes from a story or film, add the title of where it's featured here.

Add your scores in this section. The top scores are 100. Hint: make sure all characters have a weakness against other cards to make the game more fun.

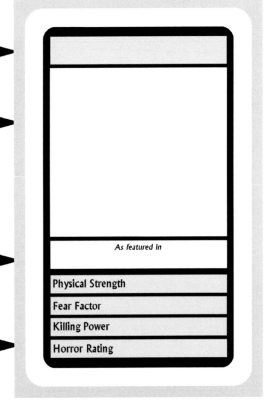

Cut out the front and back from the page and trim away the grey areas.

Glue the two sides together. Perhaps add a piece of card in the middle. Ceral box card is a good thickness for this.

Photocopy or scan the page if you don't want to cut up your Annual.

Sinister Horror Crossword

Across

1. The first book released by the Sinister Horror Company. (7,5)
4. Mitch Mooney is known better by this name. (3,3)
6. When Naomi Fuller went postal she used these to terrible effect on Kevin Doe's privates. (5)
7. Pasher tagoth _____. (4)
8. The thing that keeps Daryl awake at night. (8)
9. He opened the door to the Black Room for the second time and showed us what was in his drawers. (3,7)
11. ____ Good Girls Do. (4)
15. The deadly mercenary hunting for the Death's Head program. (6)
16. Author of Breaking Point. (3,5)
17. The Girl With The _____ Tattoo. (8)
18. & 23d. Paul Kane's failed superhero. (6,3)
21. The real name of The Chocolateman. (4)
22. Where The Bad Game is played. (5)
24. Her life was no fairy tale living in a Forest Undergound. (4)
25. Upon Waking, Cassie likes to get herself off with this. (7,5)
28. & 30. Where the manuscripts are kept. (3,5,4)
31. The brothers are far from Idol, famous for exorcising these. (6)
32. Maldicion? Say that in English! (5)

Down

1. The man that searched for clandestine delights. (3)
2. Real name of Godbomb!'s titular bomber. (5)
3. Don't be Cross at this unusual killer from The Exchange. (7)
4. Daniel Marc Chant's evil moggy. (2,11)
5. An unusual thing to have at Christmas from J. R. Park. (5,6)
10. Rich Hawkins' troubled hero that took on King Carrion. (5)
12. This cold but intangibly carnal killer will leave you Marked. (4)
13. Where J. R. Park has Death Dreams. (10)
14. Tracy Fahey's strange way of moving. (10)
19. What Daniel Marc Chant took us into. (4)
20. Described by Kayleigh Marie Edwards as a little bitey. (7)
23. (See 18 across)
26. The man behind the Sinister logo. (5)
27. Martin Powell's enraged alter ego. (5)
29. Where in Bowline does the beast live? (4)

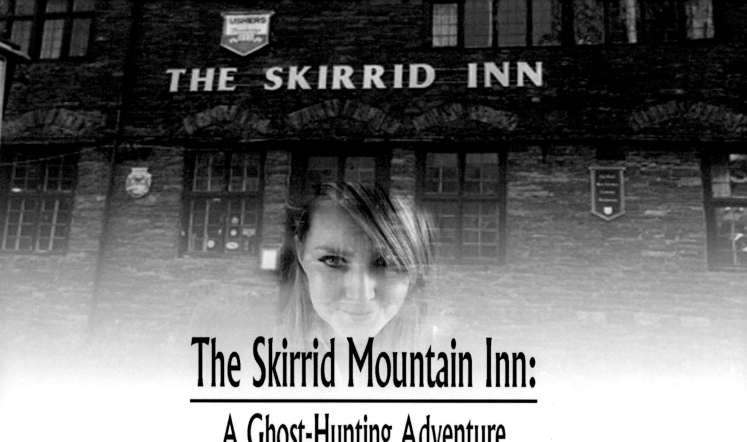

The Skirrid Mountain Inn:
A Ghost-Hunting Adventure
by Kayleigh Marie Edwards

Two years ago, I decided to take myself on a tour of Britain's most haunted locations. I planned to seize the night, welcome the demons, explore the supernatural, and fear the reaper. You know, get ghosted. I went to The Skirrid Mountain Inn for an overnight stay, located near Abergavenny in the Welsh valleys.

It is widely accepted to be one of the most haunted places in Britain. It's located next to a graveyard, and has the alleged grisly history of almost 200 people being hanged there. It would appear that death is woven into the very fabric of the place. This was the first haunted location that I went to… and it was the last.

Get ready to have your flabber ghasted, to have your gooses bumped. Prepare for my first-hand account of staying – alone – in this nightmare inn. Behold my tale of terror.

So I was driving around in the dark, swearing at myself. It was like the bloody Twilight Zone; I left in plenty of time to arrive in daylight, but my Satnav switched itself off (for no apparent reason, and it occurred to me that it could have been the work of ghosts) when I was only 2 minutes away from the location. I was driving around, lost and panicked, for like an hour before I finally found the little side road that I had to turn on to. As I parked, I thought, 'this is already like a horror film… good.. this bodes well'.

I'd love to tell you that as I approached the pub, the building loomed over me like an evil presence, but I couldn't really see it because it was too dark. There was light in the windows, and I ambled towards them like a zombie looking for live flesh. I was quite hungry you see, on account of all the driving around. I was like a moth to a flame... like David and Jack to The Slaughtered Lamb. When I entered the pub, its rustic fireplace aglow, it went silent as all of the locals turned around and stared at me. All one of them.

I was ushered in and warmly welcomed by the owners and staff, who are sincerely delightful people. They gave me the key (an actual key, not one of those modern key card malarkey things) to my room, invited me to make myself at home, and told me to just come downstairs when I wanted to order some dinner. How did they know I was hungry? Was there psychic work at play here?

Prior to my arrival, a staff member informed me that my room – Room 1 (of 3) – was the 'most haunted'. Apparently, the most activity happens in Room 1, and this is also where the most 'violent' supernatural attacks on guests happen. I had spent my life hoping to find myself plunged into my own supernatural hell. I fancied myself the sort of protagonist who would conquer all the demons, somehow find a love interest along the way, and live to see brighter days with renewed courage and wisdom. In hindsight, I was ill prepared for such a quest. I had no weaponry, had learned no incantations or banishment spells, and to be honest I didn't believe in ghosts in the first place. I thought that should something inexplicably scary happen, I'd just run outside and hide amongst the sheep. Of course, this plan was flawed. Because what if there were werewolves?

Anyway, I digress. I went up the incredibly creaky, winding stairs, and found myself outside an old, heavy, wooden door. And thus, my spooky adventure finally and truly began.

My room was gigantic, complete with a fireplace and a huge, wooden, four-poster bed. The kind of bed that people have honeymoons in. Nothing has ever reminded me more that I'm single. There were several mirrors around the place, an adjoining, freezing-cold bathroom, old furniture, and 'antiques' (you know, to give you that good old horror feel). The mirrors gave me hope, as I thought perhaps something might appear in them behind me, or my reflection might start doing weird things later on. There was also a lot of tea, which I hoped not to be haunted by because no one wants to look up into the dark and see dangling teabags.

I went about the room looking for anything spooky. I went through the drawers, I looked inside the kettle, and I even got on my hands and knees and investigated under the bed, where I actually found something. It was a balloon, a 40th birthday balloon to be exact. It reminded me of The Shining. I thought 'excellent, this bodes well'. And then I also saw a spider under there and that ruined my life for about 5 minutes because I couldn't just go down to the pub and ask someone to put it out for me. What kind of ghost hunter starts their night by being terrorised by a spider?

8-legged demon aside, there didn't seem to be anything amiss, so I ran about the room and threw cushions around and yelled insults at any ghosts that might have been lurking. Unfortunately, I got no response. No one and nothing paid any attention to me. This was also much like my single life. You know you've got absolutely no game when you go to one of the most haunted locations in the UK and even the ghost stands you up. Disgruntled, I went back downstairs in search of food.

There were a couple more customers in the pub when I got there, but I had no trouble getting a nice, little table in front of the fireplace because they had reserved it for me. I couldn't believe it. There was a little wooden 'reserved' thing on the table and everything. I thought, 'yes, this is the hobby for me'. I was practically royalty. I ordered some food and then sat there taking notes and looking through the guestbook. Everyone was staring at me like I was some big, fancy reporter. I found myself wishing that I'd had the foresight to bring a quill, instead of a regular pen. That would have really impressed them. It was great for a second until I realised something: it's off-putting when people are staring at you. Writing in a notebook is quite natural for me normally, but you try looking natural doing anything when you've got a few pairs of eyes on you. I couldn't even keep my facial expression natural because I was conscious of looking like a professional writer. What does a professional writer look like? I don't effing know, do I? I'm not a professional anything, unless you count first-place winner of a secondary school Sports Day sack race. And in the interest of full disclosure, guys, I cheated. I just put my feet in the corners and ran. I'm so ashamed.

So I'm writing away in front of a huge open fireplace. The locals are muttering around me – I couldn't hear what they were saying but I assumed they were talking about me, probably because I'm a bit narcissistic. There are these big boards on the walls telling of the grisly history of the place. Everything is old and beautiful and haunting. It's pitch black outside, and the atmosphere is heavy with its dark past. The air is full of smells; the old wood, draft ale, smoke from the fire... and fishcakes! Oh my god, the food arrived and it was everything I hoped it would be. I might have been there, alone, not yet haunted, and posing as a proper writer, but at least I had dinner. Just when I thought things couldn't get better for me, they brought out chocolate fudge cake.

Before heading back upstairs, I took note of some of the entries in the guestbook. A lot of the comments made were just along the lines of 'had a lovely stay'. However, I also found many that claimed there was supernatural activity. These claims ranged from minor hauntings like 'strange noises', and 'coughing' heard on the staircase, to violent poltergeist activity like people awakening with lamp cords wrapped around their necks, and being held under the water by an 'invisible force' in the bath. The latter accounts were mostly from people who had stayed in my room. I was practically rubbing my cake-covered hands together with glee. I couldn't wait to be haunted.

Additionally, I met a couple in the bar that were also staying overnight in Room 2. I have never seen more excited people. They were practically bursting with ghosts. They had apparently filmed 'floating orbs of light' in their room and on the staircase, and they couldn't wait for the pub to close so that the real ghost hunting could begin. I'll admit that I was intrigued. I had yet to see any floating balls myself, but it was hard to call bullshit on their orb story on account of how sincerely ecstatic they were.

I decided to head back to my room until the pub closed, but I took my time going up the staircase on my way. They've moved it, but the original beam from which people were hanged is still there. Looking at it gave me the creeps, because that was something real and very morbid. I found myself thinking about the poor people who lost their lives in that building, which is now so rustic and cosy. It was only then, as I stood motionless on that rickety, winding staircase, that the gravity of what The Skirrid Inn used to be hit me, and it was chilling. But then I remembered how nice the cake was and I was happy again.

Back in my room, I was very disappointed to find that everything was as I'd left it. I'd turned the lights off and everything, because everyone knows that ghosts do their best interfering in the dark. Disgruntled, I sat on the edge of the bed and considered the idea that I was more likely to be attacked by the couple next door than I was to see a ghost. Almost immediately after that thought had occurred to me, I saw something that froze me solid. My palms were sweaty, knees weak, arms were heavy.

That effing spider had come out from under the bed and was making its way across the wall towards my jacket, which hung on the back of a chair. The spider was much bigger than I'd first realised. I swiftly pulled the chair out from the wall and then I had an idea. Perhaps there was a ghost watching me and it just didn't quite have the strength to communicate yet. I'd seen enough horror films to realise that sometimes the ghosts gain their strength because the living believe in them. The spooky ghosties harness that belief to scare you, and the more scared you are, the more equipped they are to attack you. I did a lap of the room, casually muttering that I sure was scared and hoped nothing got me, all the while moving things around. I took the pokers from the fireplace and scattered them upright against the walls. I took some of the decorative balls out of their bowl and placed them on the corners of the table, so even a transparent entity could prod them off. I even rearranged the 'antiques', in the hope that the ghost might be attached to them in their specific places and become angered by my interference. I felt pretty good about my plan to coax out the demons. I smiled (but only on the inside, lest the ghost notice and become privy to my deceptive ways), awaiting the chaos that would ensue.

A couple of hours later, after lying in my room with the lights off, the noise in the pub downstairs dwindled and then died off completely as it closed for the night. One of the most attractive things about staying at The Skirrid is the fact that the owners are so trusting that they just lock you in and leave. I had heard this from other people who had stayed the night there, but was convinced otherwise. I was sure that they said they leave, but actually don't. I'd heard stories from past guests who claimed to hear people running around and all sorts in there, and of course, the most logical explanation for that is that the owners have you believe you're there alone, when actually they hide and intentionally scare you. I can now confirm, with absolute conviction, that this is not the case. They just leave and lock you in. Anyone that's been there can tell you that the place simply isn't big enough for a couple of adults to hide in, and there definitely isn't enough room for them to sneak past you without being seen. Believe me, I looked.

So anyway, I'm lying there in the dark and thinking of the scariest things I can to creep myself out. I hoped to scare myself enough for the ghost to pick up on my nervous energy and use it against me. I don't scare easily so it took a while. I thought of every horror film I'd ever seen. I reminisced about a really scary accident I'd been involved in. But nope, not a single goose bump. I sprawled out on the giant bed and suddenly missed my cat, and thus the terror descended. The act of missing one's cat reminds one that one is already a single cat lady, and one was still only in her twenties (just). Rigid with the weight of my own impending doom, I could feel my heart rate rise. Then... I heard the screams. Fear finally had me in its cold grip.

I sat bolt upright, the hairs on my arms rising. I was locked in, alone, in the dark. And there were screams. A big grin spread across my face as I jumped out of bed, ready to battle a transparent force or perhaps free a trapped spirit by finding its skeleton in the walls and solving a long-forgotten murder mystery. I felt like the long lost Winchester sister. Which was confusing because I also want to be a

Winchester wife. Then I heard the giggling, and remembered the couple in the next room. They were getting drunk and having a laugh. Deflated, I got up and tried to find the light switch.

I fumbled around and eventually found the light and turned it on. I squinted as the room lit up and I looked around. One of the balls from the table was on the floor, and one of the fire pokers was tipped over. This would have been very exciting if it wasn't me that had moved those items in the first place, but alas, it was. Earlier on, I'd got so bored of waiting for an entity that I'd briefly got up and flung some stuff around in the vain hope that something else would join in. Well, it didn't. This ghost hunt was starting to feel like bullshit.

On the plus side, now that the pub was empty and the owners were gone, I finally felt free to go and have a proper look at the place. I opened my bedroom door, which creaked so loudly it made me jump. I descended the first few stairs and entered a pitch-black room. The room in question used to be known as the 'prisoner cell'. It's a small space in which people sentenced to hanging had to await their fate. I couldn't find a light switch so I had to walk into the windowless room armed only with the torch on my phone. It was cold and creepy, with a ridiculously high ceiling and bare walls. Of course, it would have been creepier if it weren't also the utility closet, complete with washing machine and boxes of cleaning supplies. The ice buckets and antibacterial sprays sort of killed the vibe in there.

A noise on the staircase stopped my snooping in its tracks. There should have been no noises to hear at all; the place was empty. I heard another creak, and it was closer. There was another, and this time it was right outside the door, which stood ajar. I was genuinely terrified. I thought for sure that at any second the door would slam shut, closing out the light from the staircase and trapping me. Then I'd hear another creak, but this time it would be right next to me in the dark. This is the moment that I learned the following thing about myself; I have no fight or flight response at all. I just have a 'freeze' response. When faced with potential danger, apparently I just stand there and hope that if I don't move then maybe nothing bad will happen.

"Hello? Is someone there?" The voice was quiet and scared. Fuming, I marched out onto the staircase to find the terrified faces of the couple. They had forgotten that I was there, so of course when I left my room and went wandering around, they thought they were hearing a ghost. They looked relieved to see me, but I was beyond irritated to see them. I really thought that something had finally come to scare me. I had never been so disappointed to be among the living. I explained that I was merely conducting a ghost hunt and they thought it would be fun to join me. But I didn't agree. The whole point of staying in a haunted place alone was to get the full ghost experience. I'm not great with social awkwardness so I searched my mind for the best possible way to let them down gently. I think I settled on "fuck off please".

Alone again, I re-entered the prisoner cell. I assumed that since the door was left unlocked, it was okay to just poke through all the stuff in there, and poke I did. I mostly just found dust. But in the dust.. purely by coincidence I'm sure.. I found a Ouija board. I burst into laughter as it occurred to me that not only were the owners fine with people snooping around, but they counted on it. The Ouija Board was obviously planted there for guests to find. You can imagine how it helps business when word gets around that someone had a terrifying experience there after doing a Ouija Board – even better if it was an entire group. Group hysteria is a powerful marketing tool, especially when the experience had alcohol thrown in. I grinned at the board. Aw dammmn, shit just got real!

I put it aside for later, as I wanted to investigate first. Everything down in the pub looked different in the dark. There wasn't even light coming in through the windows; I was in the middle of nowhere in pitch black. It was almost as dark as my soul in there. I wandered around, suddenly feeling cold, and got my camera out ready to catch any activity.

Much to my surprise and delight, through my camera lens, I saw floating orbs of light. Some whizzed by, and others bumbled more slowly, but they were there. I looked up but saw nothing. But sure enough, when I looked back down at my phone screen, there they were dancing in front of me. I was excited. Orbs are a common phenomenon in haunted locations and I was thrilled to finally see something. I tried to take photographs, but nothing was caught in the pictures. Frustrated, I continued to stare through my phone screen at the floaty light balls. I stared for so long that I worked out what they were.

News just in, folks! Orbs of light are easily caught on video, sometimes captured in pictures, and very rarely seen with the naked eye, if ever. This is not because they indicate anything supernatural or paranormal, but because 'orbs' are just floating dust and lint in the air. They appear spherical and sometimes even flash because the light from your camera merely reflects off them and gives the illusion that you're seeing something more interesting than what it really is. I'm sorry if I shattered the fantasy for you but the truth demands to be told! And while I'm on a truth bender, here comes another one for you. As well as cheating in the sack race, I also Blu-tacked my egg to the spoon.

After my disappointing realisation about the orbs – which I didn't have the heart to tell the couple about but just happily shared with you - I was about to head back to my room when I realised that the only place I hadn't checked out was the men's toilets. I got as far as the door and spent a lot of time outside it before I retreated without going inside. There were two reasons for this; firstly, I can't stand the smell of urinals, and secondly, I was scared. Yep, that's right. I was too scared to go in there. I tried to push open the door and was surprised to be met with intense resistance from the other side. The door wasn't stuck on anything, and it did budge, but there was an insane draft for some reason and that made it very difficult to push the door open. I succeeded and was met with a tiny corridor and a second door, and that's where I turned back. I felt like I was in a wind tunnel, it was freezing, and I was so creeped out that I bailed on the idea. I was pretty annoyed that I'd allowed myself to get that spooked by a draft, but I figured that it was probably unlikely that I was missing out on anything in there.

I passed the couple on the stairs on the way back to my room, who were still deliriously filming 'orbs'. I closed the door behind me and sat in front of the Ouija board. Alone, I asked it the following questions;

- Is there anyone there?
- Who are you?
- Are you hostile?

After these questions, I asked more and more. I became obsessed, addicted. I was informed of many things. According to the board, I need not worry because I'm going to die a married, old lady, warm in her bed. I'll die before my husband, because that's the less boring way around to go. Before my death, I will have a long and prosperous writing career. My books will be turned into huge, fantastic,

Hollywood movies. I'll be rich and popular and envied by all. My teeth will magically go straighter. Kirsten Dunst will play me in the true movie about my life. Oh yeah, also, said husband will either be Idris Elba or Penn Badgley (the board couldn't decide).

Of course, the Ouija Board would have been a far scarier and spookier experience if my questions had actually been answered by an entity, but it was just me getting into the 'spirit' of things and pushing the glass around to the answers I wanted. What? I've already told you twice that I cheat at games.

I stayed up another couple of hours and eventually resigned myself to the reality that, as I expected, there are no such thing as ghosts. I crawled into the gigantic bed and started to doze off as I thought about the complimentary breakfast I would receive in a few hours. And that's when I heard the very loud and alarming series of bangs from the bathroom. Once again, I froze in place. I felt lucky to be already hiding under the covers. There was a moment of silence, and then I heard what sounded like footsteps. I reminded myself that the building was old, that boards creak and pipes make noises as buildings settle in the night. But I also reminded myself that the building had had hours to 'settle' and it was now verging on a new day. As I pondered my sanity, I heard what sounded like a tap turn on.

This was it. This was my chance to investigate something that actually seemed to indicate that something spooky was afoot. The longer I lay there, the more noise I heard from the bathroom. It was like the tin drummer from Slipknot was trying to launch his solo career in there. I sat up, swung my legs out of bed and then thought 'actually, nope. I've seen how this ends for people in horror films and my mamma didn't raise no fool'. I promptly swung my legs back up under the covers, lay down, and completely ignored everything else until I fell asleep.

I admit to getting totally scared right at the end there, but my overall verdict is.... No ghosts. At the beginning of this, I told you that this was my first and last stop on my ghost tour. You might have thought that what I meant by that was that I had such a terrifying time that it put me off going elsewhere. Unfortunately, that wasn't the case. The truth is that this stay, although lots of fun, just reminded me that I firmly believe that ghosts are nonsense, and I couldn't be bothered to drive anywhere else just to miss my cat.

However, The Skirrid Mountain Inn, whether you believe in ghosts or not, is a fantastic place. I'd highly recommend a stay (and/or a meal) there. It's friendly, warm, rustic, and interesting and I'd take it over a fancy hotel any time. The fact that you're left completely alone and unsupervised gives you that teenage feeling of when you got the house to yourself and had the freedom to do anything. I mean, you probably didn't do anything, but knowing you could was fun.

So to summarise, I didn't get to conquer any demons, I learned nothing, and I gained no courage. Nor did I find a love interest. In fact, I think it's actually hindered my chances because now people find me even more close-minded than I was before. So yeah, it was good. I'd give my ghost hunting adventure a score of 3 out of 2 blue pickles.

Colour in this gruesome scene from J. R. Park's Easter Hunt, a short story featured in The Offering.

engeAnce

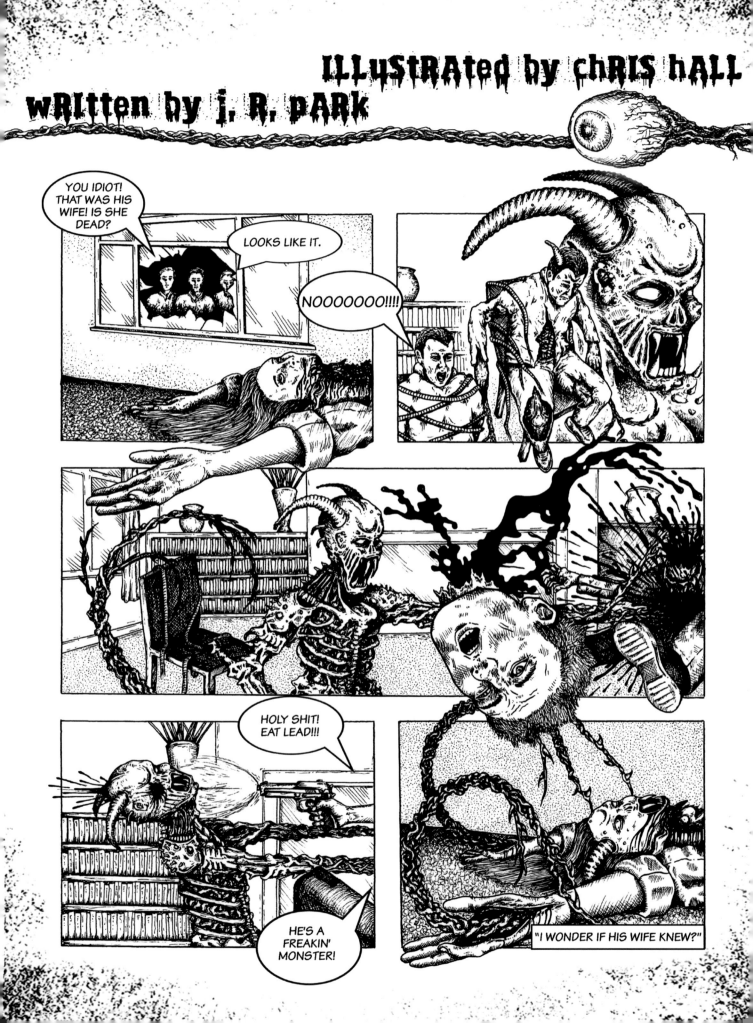

The Black Room Manuscripts:
Lost Prologue & Epilogue
by Duncan P. Bradshaw

Before Dunk left the Sinister Horror Company he was working on an anthology that would have been The Black Room Manuscripts Volume Three. That volume became the excellent Trapped Within that was published through his own EyeCue label and rasied money for the Stroke Association.

However when he first started work on the book, Dunk created a Prologue and Epilogue that continued the Black Room mythos with Dunk's own inimtable style.

Unpublished anywhere else before, and thought never to see the light of day, the Prologue and Epilogue is presented here with the kind permission of Duncan P. Bradshaw.

Prologue

It was hot, damn hot. I'm talking full on, wrapped up in a coat, balaclava, three hats, hugging a radiator, sitting on the sun kinda hot.

Hell, if this insufferable heatwave was a thing, it would be a financially astute stripper. Using all of the cash thrust into their sequined thong, to buy a two floor property in the city centre, turning it into a video game arcade by day, and a bar and music venue at night. That was how hot it was.

So I'm sitting there in just my pants, all the windows flung open to the extremes of their hinges, fan on full blast, aimed directly at me. It doesn't make one jot of difference, as the only air that's being moved around, is the same sweaty humid air that's been hanging around for the best part of a month already.

I barely had the energy to hydrate myself anymore. I was on the verge of opening the fridge freezer yet again, to bask in its icy, bollock cooling tendrils - to hell with the wife's protestations - when I heard it.

That off kilter melody, borne aloft on the stagnant meagre breeze. Could it be? Surely not. It must be a mirage, an auditory prank on my feeble senses. But it grew louder, and louder. Peeling myself from the leather armchair, which had become my summer tomb, I walked over to the window.

Kids played in the street, seemingly oblivious to the heatwave which had laid everyone else low. Not one of their faces acknowledged the tinkling jaunty tune. I was about to return to my sweat stained chair, now convinced that it was but a figment of my melting brain, when I saw it.

It was like no ice cream van I had ever seen. Just a plain white box van, an old fashioned bullhorn speaker fixed above the cab, blaring out that discordant song. What was it? It sounded familiar, but every attempt to pin down what popular song it was, evaded me, just at the point of its capture.

Like a zombie, I staggered outside, having raided the coffee table of all of my change. By god, I'd give all of it away, the princely sum of £4.74, and a strip of spearmint chewing gum, just to have an ice lolly.

Why stop there? my brain said.

Why not go the full hog, and have a ninety-nine?

With a flake.

A fucking flake!

How the hell would it last in this infernal heat?

My mind had obviously turned to mulch.

FOCUS ON THE ICE CREAM VAN.

As my feet slapped down on the tarmac, it felt slick, like it was on the verge of melting away to a thick sludge. If I had any bacon left, which hadn't spoiled from the fridge being left open to cool my wretched body, I would see if it would cook on the pavement.

I got to the front of the van, but could see no serving hatch along its flank. This must be a trick of the mind, the heat playing yet another jolly jape on my addled brain. By now, I was angry, the one solace on this sweltering day, had been denied to me.

By jove, I would find out what their ruddy game was.

I bashed my fist on the passenger door, looking in to see three men looking back at me. The driver had grey spiky hair, with matching stubble, the middle one had dyed black hair, also spiked, a piercing in his eyebrow.

The passenger, a man with a shaved head and sporting gaudy tattoos on his arms, wound the window down, seemingly to berate me. But nothing came hither. I looked closer, each was uttering a singular soundless word, in sequence, starting with the driver, through to the passenger. Once the Mexican wave of miming was complete, they started again, in perfect synchronicity.

'What are you saying?' I demanded. I got no reply. I was on the verge of storming off, when the skinhead leant through the window, mouthed his word, then thumbed to the rear of the vehicle.

'Is it ice cream?' I asked.

Nothing.

I should've known better than to go there. You know that, don't you? I should've hopped, skipped and jumped up the pathway, my feet blistering from the heat, slammed the door, and reattached myself back in my armchair.

But I didn't. As I walked towards the rear, I heard the window thud closed on the passenger side. I cast a quick glimpse into the wing mirror, and saw they were all still there, mouthing their mysterious phrase.

At the back of the van, was a door, slightly ajar. I wondered how they could've been driving around with it in that state. Surely it would've flown open? Carefully, I pulled on the handle...

It opened up into a long dark corridor, lit by flaming torches.

How could this be? Perhaps I had been driven mad by the constant heat and lack of sleep. Maybe I was dead already, and this was but the portal to the otherworld.

I could see a door at the end of the hall. Lecherous faces carved onto its surface, illuminated by the flickering light. It lured me in, tempting me with knowledge, and answers to questions I hadn't even formed or considered.

Once inside the corridor, I looked behind me, to see that the world had shrunk away. The children played on regardless, the van and I not even registering on their spectrum. I edged towards the door, the swirling faces changed appearance with every flicker of waning torchlight.

Finally, I reached it, I ran my hand down the contorted facial features. As I did, the black from its surface ran along my fingers, and up my arm. I twisted the door knob, revealing a vast chamber within. Bookshelves ran from floor to ceiling, which in itself, disappeared into the heavens above.

A pedestal stood proudly in front of me, upon it lay a single tome, covered in thick bound black leather. I can't explain it, it was like I was meant for it, and it me. Sigils and angular lines ran over its cover, I undid the thick metal clasp, and opened it, ready to receive the words contained within…

Epilogue

What madness!

What delight and rapture!

The words, they felt so real back then, they comforted me like a milk maid, slashed me like a whip, raked my soul like a wraith. But what did they mean? I stumbled from the van, out into the world. The heat, replaced by arctic cold, virginal snow lay all around. Stars twinkled in the sky above, my breath adding to the thin clouds which ambled in the heavens.

Bodies lay all around me. Men, women, children. Their throats slit, blood red ties printed on the pristine snow, as if their souls had evacuated through the ragged wound. Snow lightly covered their form, they had been here for some time.

But who did this?

When was this?

I had been gone but moments, or so it seemed.

I looked down to my hand and saw that I was holding a knife, its blade curved like a crescent moon. The blood was fresh, crimson droplets pitter pattered onto the white blanket, sizzling through the snow, to the concrete beneath.

I staggered to the front of the cab, I must get answers. I had to know the truth. If these murders are my doing, then I should at least discover what the motive was. Every step I took ended in a crunch, as I trampled the lightly packed snow underfoot.

The passenger window was closed, the three men inside unchanged, maintaining their wordless incantation, staring into the future with uncaring eyes. I pounded my fists on the window, the skinhead looked at me, and wound the window down.

'Tell me!' I demanded. 'Tell me what I witnessed inside that infernal place. All those words, all those thoughts, what were they? What have they done to me? What have you done to me?'

As one, they ceased their silent chanting, and looked at me. Each birthed a smirk, exchanging knowing glances. Then, from driver through to the passenger, they enunciated their words aloud.

'Pasher.'

'Tagoth.'

'Imra.'

I staggered backwards, I had heard that phrase before, when I was lost in that library, that damned place of insanity and fools.

They recanted the words once more.

'Pasher.'

'Tagoth.'

'Imra.'

I pawed at my face, tore at my cheeks, 'Tell me what it means,' I implored.

'Pasher.'

'Tagoth.'

'Imra.'

With the final word spoken, they smiled at me. The passenger window closed shut. The three figures looked forwards. The engine spluttered into life, and the van pulled away.

As I stood there, watching the van disappear around the corner, I sunk to my knees, amongst the fallen seeds of my victims. Had I really done this? Surely it was the words, wasn't it? It couldn't have been me. It was them, the three of them.

They did this.

To me.

To them.

Not me.

It couldn't have been me.

Could it?

From the corner of the street, came not the sound of the ice cream van, but of sirens.

Desperate.

Keening.

The sound bored into my skull like a low powered drill. I looked down to the sharp blade, still bleeding into the snow. I knew what I had to do. What needed to be done. To close the deal. Seal the pact.

I ran the blade slowly across my throat, and waited for the secrets of that black room, to be bestowed on me once more.

What if Lego got nasty and made Sinister Horror Sets...

18+
SHC012
Gēmuōbā
Teen Attack

18+
SHC013
Bitey Bachman
Hospital
Massacre Set

18+
SHC014
Issac
The Bomber

SINISTER HORROR COMPANY

NOT **LEGO**

18+

SHC015

Room 6
Stand-off Set

LYDIAN FAUST

FOREST UNDERGROUND

SINISTER HORROR COMPANY

NOT **LEGO**

in association with

EyeCue Productions

18+

SHC016

Dana And
The Entity

PRIME DIRECTIVE

DUNCAN P. BRADSHAW

SINISTER HORROR COMPANY

NOT **LEGO**

18+

SHC017

Kiko And Mark
Black Plant Set

MARKED

STUART PARK

Spot The Difference: Can you find the 6 differences in each cover?

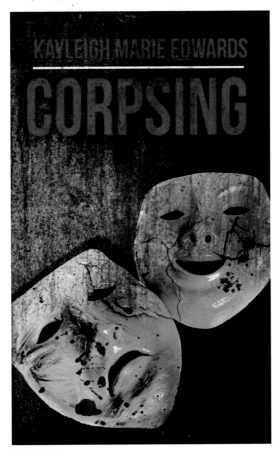

KAYLEIGH MARIE EDWARDS

CORPSING

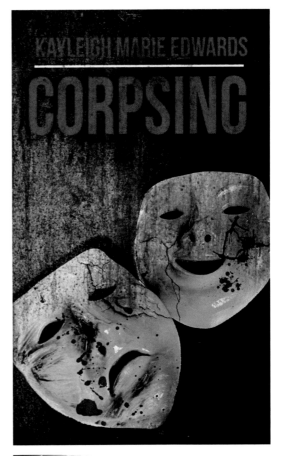

KAYLEIGH MARIE EDWARDS

CORPSING

MARKED

STUART PARK

MARKED

STUART PARK

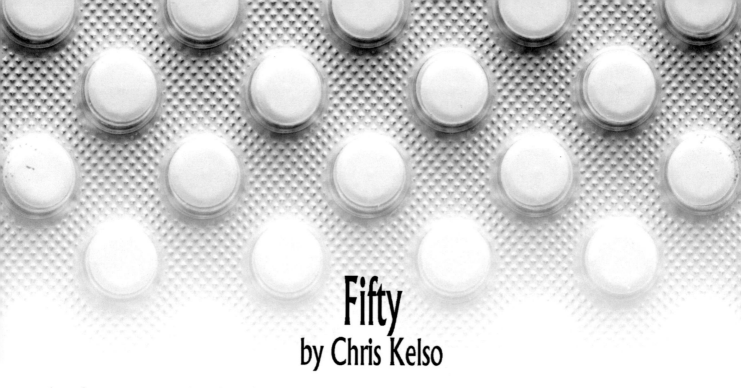

Fifty
by Chris Kelso

Ipso-facto - everyone lives by selling something. The council have been selling ex-cons like me into slavery for decades. I'm a number now. Can't complain though. Really, I can't.

Two years ago, the council pulled me out of Road-Kill collection, assigned me to working in Memory-Cutting. No idea why - must've seen something in me. Maybe I've paid my dues. It's an easy job, Memory-Cutting. Pay is decent for a council income.

Just for selling people amnesia capsules.

For being a state-funded drug-dealer.

There's a lot invested in these little tabs of oblivion, mind you. And, hey, I'm in a good racket. I'm grateful. My mother is proud for sure.

Glasgow: Some sooty precinct, Cyldeside. I do enjoy a home-town job. Makes me appreciate the warmer climates when I get them, know what I mean? - if only I could help the city forget Charles Rennie McIntosh and Alexander 'Greek' Thomson.

Still.

The man code-named: 'Mr Giro', appears at the bottom of the street wearing orange council waterproofs. Looks like everyone else in this city, like a starving proletariat ghost. A sad little slum-rat-of-a-man. He comes into the asbestos-light. Papery skin lain over deep angles of bone.

God, this used to be me.

I reach out, shake his trembling hand. Damp. Steel-cold.

Addict?

We enter the cooperative-building illuminated by LED lights, council branch-no.49. Giro eyeballs me as we walk up the stairway side-by-side.

He tries to smile.

'Good to finally meet you.' I say, awkwardly. 'Your e-mails were vague.'

'It's better to give specifics in person.' – Giro replies with haunted uncertainty. In that moment we share a synapse of recognition. Dejavu building like bees in prime swarm - then disperses. I'm sure standing face-to-face in our identical council waterproofs we look like a mirror-image of the same broken, West of Scotland man.

'Have we met?' – I ask him.

He shakes his head – no.

Fair enough.

But Mr Giro keeps eyeballing me. He has these dipped eyes. The sad eyes of an ex-con, of someone who's just a number now. In a former life we probably did jobs together, ran in similar circles. Poor guy must've got a bad gig. Corpse-handler or a County Cutthroat. Something brutal. As I say, I'm grateful I got a decent hand.

'I always wanted to be a Memory-Cutter. You're lucky. I get redeployed allthedamntime.' – He says, spreading himself on the office couch like a recumbent statue - 'Listen, I'm about to do something terrible. I can feel it. I don't know what it is yet, but I know I won't want to remember any of it, okay?'

'Okay.'

I've heard it all before. Blah, blah, blah. They've all done terrible things or about to do terrible things. Ex-cons, doctors, coppers, and stay-at-home-mums. Thieves, killers, paedophiles, cheats, and liars. Just like everyone else in this big icy universe, there's always someone who needs to forget their own nature. But this isn't the time to cogitate. I need to make the sale. Quotas to be met and all that.

Aye...

Industry axiom: 'The difference between involvement and commitment is like ham and eggs. The chicken is involved; the pig is committed.'

I start my schpeel:

'First, let me put your mind at ease. Our product is synthesised and sourced locally, right here in Glasgow...'

Truth: Our product is synthesised in Amsterdam labs by mechanical-behemoths, sourced in the ethically-bankrupt human-testing facilities of southern China.

I go on -

'See, the pill destroys neurons and proteins, rewires connections between memory and emotion. It's very much full-proof. Better still, it's guaranteed to permanently remove bad memories. We can implant new ones for you as well. Nice ones, in pill-form. Just an extra thirty.'

Truth: It destroys neurons and proteins, sure - but it's far from "full-proof". Nothing can be guaranteed. Reconsolidation of memories remains entirely possible. All it takes is the right trigger - a phrase, an image, a number. Still, they're hardly going to put that in the advertising campaign, are they? I'm a salesman forchristsakes.

'I don't want new memories,' he says, 'I just need enough to get rid of what I'm going to do.'

'You're positive you don't want something new in there before I go? It's very reasonably priced. Council discount.'

He's having none of it. Commitment. I don't want to miss an opportunity with this guy. Vulnerability makes him exploitable – another industry saying.

'See, a gap in recall might lead your future self to become suspicious and attempt a self-re-wiring, to explain the unaccountable timeline blip.'

'I thought it was full-proof?' – He says, looking at me sceptically out the corner of his eye.

'Come on, nothing is completely full-proof.'

You can't sell a doughnut without acknowledging the hole, right?

'I don't have an extra thirty.'

Let it go. Don't be too pushy. Might frighten him away.

'Well, I'm not much of a writer anyway. I'll give you enough to re-arrange the old filing cabinets, okay? That'll be forty large.'

Giro sits up, pulls a wad of crushed notes from the back-pocket of his Levi's.

'Here.' – He says.

I take the notes, fan them. Smell them. Crunch them between my palms. Forty large. Mr Giro seizes the blister pack of memory-erasing drugs and pops two of the blue pills into his shaking palm.

'Ah, see, you'll have to wait till you're off council-property before you take those. You know how funny they get about that stuff when it happens in their own backyard.'

He just looks at me gravely. I notice on the back of one of the bills there's something written in blue biro- 'Fifty'.

'Fifty,' I say, 'What's fifty?'

Mr Giro's eyes glaze over as if the number has activated something in his mind. Zombified, he reaches into his Levi's, produces a long-barrel pistol - council-standard issue. He pumps the slide-stop, rests his thumbs over the hammer. The nozzle is placed to my forehead.

'I'm sorry.' He says. 'Consider yourself redeployed.'

What if Lego got nasty and made Sinister Horror Sets...

18+
SHC018
Roman Monster Set

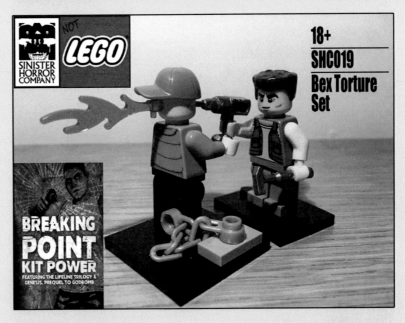

18+
SHC019
Bex Torture Set

18+
SHC020
Kreb Choc-Choc Set

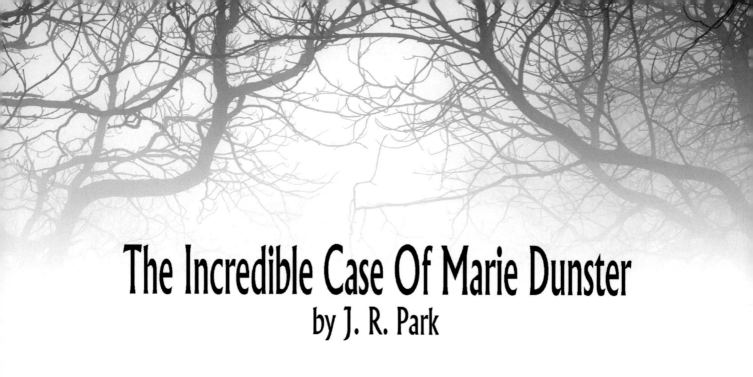

The Incredible Case Of Marie Dunster
by J. R. Park

The blue and green dome leant at an angle; evidence of the haste and inexperience with which the tent had been erected. Light winds shook the canvas, causing it to vibrate against the breeze, but its waterproof shell remained taut between the carbon rods, keeping the cold October weather at bay.

A torch light glowed from inside the tent creating strange silhouettes. The two inhabitants giggled from within the canvas confines, their shadows spilled across the grass and onto the surrounding trees.

'Achingly hard?' Marie quizzed, unsuccessfully hiding both her shock and amusement.

'You said talk dirty,' Charlie answered, pulling her closer to him as they lay together underneath an unzipped sleeping bag, surrounded by a plethora of empty wine bottles.

'I know, but achingly hard.' She smiled as she turned and looked into her lover's eyes. Her dark hair was matted and ruffled from lying down, and smelt of the bonfire they'd made earlier. 'I ask you, what does that even mean?'

'When you have a dick the size of mine,' he said pulling her even closer so their two bellies sandwiched his erection, 'then when it gets hard — I mean really hard, like how you make me — then it aches. It hurts. But in a good way.'

She smiled as she admired the contours of his face. It had been a year since they'd first started dating, but unlike the normal course of her relationships, the spark was still there. In fact she might dare say it had grown brighter. Every day they laughed. Every day was an adventure. Spontaneity kept the excitement alive, and although Marie was a little hesitant about camping in the autumn to celebrate their anniversary together, Charlie's smile and sense of excitement never failed to win her over.

Reaching below the covers, Marie gently squeezed his cock in her palm. Its girth felt rigid. Strong. She bit her bottom lip as she brought it closer to her damp crotch. Despite his clumsy come on, his good looks and chiselled body were too hot to ignore. As was his penis.

'I know about the size of your cock giving pain — in a good way.' A dirty smile spread across her face.

Charlie gasped as Marie directed his swollen member. Teasing it across her labia for a moment, she closed her eyes and thrust her pelvis forward, waiting for the rush of pleasure as his cock filled her completely.

Her boyfriend groaned as he slid inside, feeling her vagina grip him with practiced precision. His fingers gripped onto her and squeezed her arms. Marie threw her head back; with her eyes shut she had no distractions. Her sole focus was purely on the feeling. The pleasure.

Charlie groaned again; louder. His rhythmic pumping increasing until it hit a steady tempo. She arched her back, allowing his penis to hit her g-spot. The pleasure built inside of her, growing as she licked her own fingers and placed the moistened tips on her clitoris. Marie's other hand gripped Charlie's firm ass, and felt it tense with each pelvic thrust.

She opened her legs wider, encouraging him to sink deeper and deeper into her.

Without warning, his rhythm faltered. Unusually, Charlie fell out of time, losing the beat as his once measured motion of passion turned into something more erratic; a primitive, wild thrashing. His grip strengthened on her body. His clench tightened and began to hurt. Charlie's pitch grew higher; louder. Groans escalated to screams that in turn heightened to a barely legible:

'Heeelllllpppppp mmmmeeee Maaarrrieeee!'

Her eyes flew open, as she tore herself aware from her rapture, to see his face; a face filled with terror! With a sudden jolt he began sliding out of the tent as if someone was pulling at his legs. Reaching out, he grabbed hold of his girlfriend's arms, interlocking fingers and pulling Marie upright. Leaning backwards, she tried to hold her ground, doing all she could to keep him inside the tent.

'What's happening?' Marie screamed.

Charlie tried to answer, but his wails of anguish stole his response.

'I can't hold on!' Marie cried, her arms straining against the force of their mysterious aggressor.

Digging her heels into the ground, she pulled with all her might. Charlie began to shake, his features convulsed and twitched independently of each other. A white wisp of smoke trickled from his nostrils, steadily increasing until plumes of thick vapour shot, like steam from a kettle, out of every orifice.

Marie tried to scream, to vent her disgust, but her abhorrence kept her silent. An amazed, morbid fascination mixed with her revulsion as she watched Charlie's eyeballs bubble in their sockets before slowly dribbling in rivulets down his face.

The bubbling, white liquid dripped onto her legs as she found the air to scream; to call for help. The place was quiet, secluded. That's exactly why they came here in the first place. She knew there'd be no one around to answer her cries, but it didn't stop her from trying.

Tears ran down her face as the futility set in.

A jolt shot through her body like the bite of an electric fence, and she released her boyfriend. His arms and head dropped to the ground as he continued to spasm. Charlie looked towards her with a featureless face, and as he weakly opened his mouth in an attempt to speak, the remains of his charcoaled tongue fell to the ground. The pathetic black piece of smouldering flesh was scorched dry, fragmenting as it hit the floor.

Stunned for a moment, Marie sat in silence and looked at the charred cheeks of her lover.

'Charlie?' she whispered meekly.

Unsure whether he was alive or dead, Marie reached towards him; to check for a response upon her touch. Trying to quietly sniff back the tears that continued to roll down her face, Marie's fingertips were inches away when she stopped and jumped back, fearing for her safety. His corpse was suddenly pulled away; dragged by his feet by something unseen, into the darkness.

The smoke rolled up past Marie's cheeks and drifted towards the ceiling. Her face looked emotionless; her mouth straight, her cheeks rock-still and her eyes hidden behind dark lenses.

It was unusual to wear sunglasses at such a time, but given the circumstances she had been allowed the grace of the questioning detective.

A little bit of comfort might help her talk.

'It was like he'd been zapped by some kind of freakin' cattle prod.' She spoke as she exhaled plumes from her lungs.

Marie dropped her cigarette into a plastic cup and listened to the cold coffee sizzle as hot ash hit the cool liquid. The table wobbled on uneven legs as she rested her elbows on its surface.

'And you didn't see anything else?' Detective Lamb quizzed.

Marie lifted her elbows and let the table fall back to its original position. The thud as it hit the floor echoed in her head louder than it did in the room. She clenched her teeth in annoyance and lit another cigarette.

'You know we don't normally allow smoking in here,' the detective told her.

'Really.' She looked over the top of her sunglasses and into his eyes. 'I guess that makes me a lucky girl.'

Marie watched the flame catch, igniting the end of her Malboro. Placing her lighter on the table, the weight caused the desk to wobble for a moment; its legs rattling against the floor, back and forth like a fallen coin until it finally came to rest.

She knew it had happened. She could see it replaying in her mind. Her boyfriend pulled from her embrace and torched like a barbequed burger right in front of her eyes.

As she took a long, slow drag on her cigarette she knew how she should be feeling, and yet there was no sadness; no grief. Her eyes felt dry, bathed in the smoke that surrounded her. Where were the tears?

She eyed up Detective Lamb's tie, annoyed that it sat crooked, then gently ground her teeth as she looked at the table between them. The table leg on her closest left was suspended in the air. Was the floor wonky? Who would make a wonky floor? Then it must be the table. Why would you make a wonky table? Why hasn't anyone put anything under it to level it out? Surely she wasn't the first person to notice this. This wasn't a new table. This couldn't be a new problem that only just materialised as she was led into the interview room. What was wrong with these people?!

'Ms Dunster,' the detective momentarily freed her from her thoughts. 'Can you tell us anything that happened to you? You've been missing for four days.'

'I remember trees,' she replied truthfully, leaving the sentence hanging in the proceeding silence.

Leaning back on the table, the quiet was broken by the thud of its legs as they pivoted on their imbalance; the closest one to her left, slamming to the floor.

Detective Lamb sighed as he sat back at his desk. Marie Dunster was a difficult one. Either her mind had been blanked from some kind of emotional trauma or she was withholding information. He'd seen cases like this before; cases where witnesses showed no emotion, at least not the kind you would expect. Some gentle coercing from a counsellor had been known to unlock the floodgates. To let the information come spilling out amongst a torrent of tears and anger.

Of course that might not be the case. She might be as guilty as sin. Maybe she killed her boyfriend, accidentally or not, and then got lost in the woods. She seemed smart; smart enough to know that fake responses would be seen through. Crocodile tears were easily dried and even easier to spot.

He sighed again, allowing his breath to exhale slowly like Ms Dunster had done during the interview.

It had been seven years since he smoked his last roll up, but as he rubbed his stubbly chin he fantasised about inhaling deeply on a cigarette.

'Catch you later, Lamb,' a voice called out.

He looked up to see Detective Howard leaving; a selection of Halloween masks in his hand. Lamb smiled as he thought back to how his kids used to love this time of year. How they used to get dressed up after school and wait for their Dad. He would take pride in dressing up with them – Frankenstein's monster being his personal costume of choice – and escorting them through the town, knocking on everyone's door that had an illuminated Jack O'Lantern glowing fiendishly in the window.

His sons, Alex and Noah, really loved Halloween: the sweets, the masks and make up, the laughs. He hoped they still did; it had been so long since he'd seen them. The occasional Skype call from Australia was all his ex-wife would allow.

Two years, and the pain hadn't dulled.

The detective leant forward and picked up a small tube of superglue. He needed to clear his mind; get some focus. They had twenty four hours to hold Marie Dunster. They had to make it count. With a set of tweezers in his other hand he delicately picked up a small, grey stone and smeared a measured blob of the adhesive to one edge. Hunching over a small diorama, he carefully placed the stone into an exact position; pushing it firmly onto the green flock that covered the miniature hills of his model scene. Lamb sat back and admired his creation. Slowly but surely his replica of a prehistoric Stonehenge was coming to life.

He smiled, admiring his patient craftsmanship and began feeling instantly calmer. One more piece and he'd get back to work with a mind free from the thoughts of his failed marriage and the craving for cancer sticks.

With uniform precision he repeated his steps by picking up a small, grey stone with his tweezers and applying superglue carefully to its base. Leaning back over his model, he selected its place and reached forward, carefully hovering the piece over its designated place in the miniature model.

Suddenly the ground around him shook and the lights flickered. Lamb fell forward, dropping the stone, but managing to stop himself from crashing, chest first, onto the desk. The disturbance ended as abruptly as it came.

What the hell was that? he thought. An earthquake? Here?

Confused and shaken, he was momentarily relieved when he saw his model still standing. The relief, however, was short lived when a scream echoed down the corridor.

Getting to his feet and following the sound, Detective Lamb found himself running towards the holding cells. Stopping at cell three he was shocked to discover the door ripped from its hinges and smashed to pieces, scattered on the floor with the guarding officer sprawled out on the ground looking equally as broken.

'What happened?' Lamb asked crouching down beside the wounded police officer. 'Are you oka-?'

He stopped as he saw his colleague's face, or at least what was left of it. With half his jawbone torn from his cheek and dangling uselessly on slivers of flesh, the pain was ebbing at his consciousness. The officer tried to speak, but blood poured from an open wound across his neck, soaking his uniform and staining it a deep red.

'Ssshhh now,' Lamb spoke softly as he fumbled for his phone to call an ambulance, trying his best to hide the disgust he felt looking at his colleague's terrible injuries.

He glanced into cell three, and felt his heart sink further. It was empty.

Even with all the adrenaline that coursed through his body, Detective Lamb could think clearly enough to recall exactly who'd occupied that cell: he'd spent the last hour speaking to their blank, uncaring face.

It was Marie Dunster's cell.

And she was missing.

Faces came out of the growing darkness, twisted and horrific.

As Marie staggered through the town, she took a meandering path, unsure of where she was headed, as long as it was away from the plume of smoke that billowed from the police station.

Dazed and confused, the escapee found herself on the edge of a residential area. The red brick houses and neatly trimmed lawns were a contrast to the hordes of children that ran down the street, dressed as devils, zombies and witches.

Their masks confused Marie at first; startled by their monstrous appearances it took her some time to realise it must have been Halloween.

She sat on a wall and tried to get her bearings.

What had happened? How did she escape the cell?

Her head was a jumble of thoughts; fragments of images and memories that slewed together creating an un-cohesive college. A bug-eyed mask made of painted egg boxes and papier-mâché broke through her clouded recollections. Marie's back stiffened as the alien visage viewed her with six unblinking pupils made of pasta and pen lids. She knew it was nothing more than a child's mask, yet something about it pulled at her mind; an uncomfortable feeling like fingernails being dragged down the inside of her skull.

'Trick or treat!' came the muffled voice of an eight year old.

Marie stared blankly as her hands pulsed with a strange energy.

'Got any candy?' the child asked holding out his plastic cauldron already half full with chocolate coins, sugar lollies and jelly snakes.

A hunger gripped Marie, a desire to tear and rend; to pull the child limb from limb, sever his flesh from bone and drink his young blood.

Her hands itched with an invisible force, a longing to destroy. She reached forward to twist his neck.

'George,' a soft call floated through the air. 'George, come here and stop bothering that nice lady.'

The boy instantly responded, turned and ran towards his mother, evading Marie's murderous grasp by mere moments. He laughed with glee as he sprinted down the street, his arms held out at his sides mimicking an aeroplane, oblivious to the threat he'd unwittingly avoided.

The chatter and giggles pierced her brain. Marie felt her senses sharpen; sounds and smells flooded her thoughts. Each sensation deepening her destructive desires. Rising to her feet she stumbled into the shadows, leaving suburbia as she found solace beneath the towering structures of the nearby factories.

Resting in an alleyway, she leant back against a cold, brick wall and lit a cigarette. With all the workers already left for the day, the place was quiet. She basked in the tranquillity as she tried to make sense of the day's events.

The police interview. The holding cell.

The poorly spelt graffiti on the walls.

Waiting for a phone call from her solicitor.

Darren loves Sharon 4eva.

The eyes of the policeman through the cell door staring at her. Leering.

That feeling, the same as brought on by the child in the Halloween mask.

Then what?

Just black.

An explosion.

Smoke. Alarms.

Suddenly she's on the street.

Running.

'Got a spare smoke?' A voice slurred in the dusk.

Marie looked over the top of her sunglasses and studied the frame of a slender figure walking towards her. The closer he came, the more she could make out his tattered clothes, ripped and stained. A wild, ginger beard sprouted from his chin, matted together from morsels of food, spilt whiskey and saliva that dribbled from a crooked mouth.

It was already dark as the long evening staked its claim on the remaining hours of the day. Detective Lamb drove around the streets, his radio on and his eyes peeled, looking for the escapee.

Children were already walking from house to house, knocking on doors and asking for sweets whilst dressed in the most gruesome costumes their imaginations and artistic skills could muster. Miniature werewolves laughed with pygmy witches as they swung pumpkin shaped bags of sugary bounty, walking hand in hand.

Lamb had alerted the mayor of the incident in the station. It was up to him to call a curfew or not. If he'd had it didn't seem like the message had got through.

'Detective Lamb,' the radio crackled. 'Looks like we've found Ms Dunster. Seems she encountered a spot of bother in the alley outside Sims Chemicals.'

'Go on,' Lamb radioed back.

'Our local, open-air resident, Mental Mike had taken one too many sips of the moonshine and took a liking to her.'

'Is she okay?' he enquired.

'Ms Dunster? She's shaken but safe,' came the reply. 'As for Mike, well it seems Ms Dunster ran and he gave chase. The poor bastard must have staggered out into the street and got hit by a car. Ms Dunster says it was a hit and run. Chief, you should see the state of him.'

'Christ,' Lamb sighed. 'Ms Dunster told you all of this?'

'Yeah. She seems a lot more talkative than before.'

'Keep her there and record what she's saying. I'm coming over.'

The Detective thumped the steering wheel. They'd got her. Perhaps the fresh attack had dislodged something. If she was talking it was best not to disturb her, just listen to what she said before getting her back to the station.

Turning on his siren he made a U-turn in the road and sped towards the industrial sector, heading to Sims Chemicals.

He made the distance in no time, turning the siren and lights off as he approached his colleague's car; he didn't want anything to spook Marie.

What was she saying? What had happened at the station? Ms Dunster was not capable of breaking through a cell door and pulling a man's face off. There had to be someone else doing this. An accomplice? Or perhaps someone was after her.

The question was who?

What kind of trouble was she in?

It was dark as he approached the car. Dark and silent.

Turning on a torch he saw the familiar colours of the squad car, and made out a silhouette standing next to it. The shape suggested a head of long hair running down their back.

'Ms Dunster? Is that you?' Detective Lamb called out. 'Where are my colleagues? Where's Oakland and Smith?'

The figure didn't answer and remained silent, not even turning to acknowledge him.

Lamb stepped closer, shining the torch around the area.

'Ms Dunster?' he tried again. 'Marie? It's okay. Who's after you? We're here to help.'

The detective stumbled as he fell into an unseen puddle. Shining his torch toward his feet, the puddle looked black. From the edge of the water he saw a piece of rope trail along the ground. Following the knotted vine he quickly realised he wasn't looking at a piece of rope at all, but something far more organic; something far more human.

The intestine ended in a coil next to a strange bloodied sack. His mind thought back to the last time he'd seen something so foul, during his days in training when he was an eager recruit. The shock of the horrific pictures he'd been shown back then were meant to harden him to such sights, but as bile climbed his throat he knew it hadn't worked.

As he looked past the disembowelled stomach, the ground came alive with colour. A deep, blood-red liquid saturated the ground and soaked torn scraps of clothing that littered the floor. A stab vest lay in pieces; Smith's radio still clipped to the front, his severed hand clutching at the blood splattered device.

Trying not to be sick, Detective Lamb shone the light back towards the figure in a hope to find some answers. The illumination revealed the face of Marie Dunster as she slowly turned to face him. Her mouth dripped with crimson liquid as she held the decapitated head of PC Oakland in her hands. Taking a bite into the features of his lifeless face she pulled at the still warm flesh and tore a chunk off his cheek; cracking bone between her teeth as she did so.

Her eyes seemed to glow in the torch light like a cat's. She dropped the head as Detective Lamb approached, fumbling for his pepper spray.

'Hold it right there,' he called out, shocked in disbelief. Not knowing, himself, what he was doing; his mind twisted to the point of snapping. All he had to hold on to was his duty. 'Ms Dunster, you're under arrest.'

She hissed and spat, before turning and with incredible agility, scaled the chain link fence beside her.

Jumping at the escaping woman, Detective Lamb failed to catch her foot. He clutched at the fence himself but couldn't find the strength or grip to haul himself up.

Shining the torch through the wire, he watched as the figure ran through the fields and into the surrounding woods.

Back towards the campsite.

Towards the place they'd found her.

The grass should have felt wet under her feet, but as Marie ran through the fields it didn't feel like she was touching the ground at all.

The night air was soothing as it rushed past her face. She had to reach the trees, to find safety.

What is happening to me? she screamed in her own head; but still no tears came. What have I done?

She remembered the dismemberment of the tramp and police officers with crystal clear detail. The feeling of their bones snapping within her grip. The taste of their meat as she sunk her teeth into their necks, chewing at the skin until it split open and released hot geysers of blood into her mouth. It would be a lie if she said she'd felt controlled, if she felt like someone else was making her do those terrible things: making her eat their flesh. The truth was she wanted to do it; wanted nothing more at that moment than to destroy, rend and tear.

What happened to Charlie? What happened to me? Where was I for all those days?

Marie searched for answers, but all she found was 'trees'.

Head to the trees, her mind screamed at her. You killed those people! You ate their skin; and you loved it! What is wrong with you? Why won't you feel anything? Why won't you cry?

As the treeline rapidly approached she realised she was galloping towards it, but not on her hands and feet. Her hands were stretched out in front of her, her feet behind like she was laid out horizontally.

As she understood what was happening, she realised it would have made her feel sick.

If she could feel anything at all.

It hadn't taken long to round up a task force. Cop killers in any jurisdiction were quickly hunted down and caught. The atrocity of these Halloween killings had stirred up a bloodlust amongst the force. Vengeance made their trigger fingers keen and itchy. Tonight the guns were shared round, even Detective Lamb gleefully took hold of a pistol.

The dogs barked, straining at their leashes at the edge of the wood.

'Alright,' Lamb called order to the men and women that had answered his call. Winters, Digby, Davenport, Roberts and Briggs. 'Tonight is pretty unusual to say the least. But you've all seen the mess.'

'We want to kick some ass!' Davenport screamed with a wild holler.

'You've seen what was left of your friends after Marie Dunster was finished with them,' Lamb continued ignoring the cry, but thankful for the enthusiasm. 'We've got a real nasty one on the loose. A real wacko.'

'You god damn right!' Digby cut in. 'Real fucking loon.'

'If we can capture her alive that's great,' Lamb explained.

Boos came from the baying group.

'Let's keep it professional, peeps,' Lamb responded with a smile that betrayed the sentiment of his words. 'But if we have to use our weapons... one way or another this motherfucker is going down.'

The small army cheered, proudly holding their firearms in the air as a salute to the Detective.

With his speech finished the dogs were let off their leashes and sprinted into the darkness of the tree covered surroundings. The police officers followed behind, rushing through the wood like a group of eager school children all chasing a football.

Lamb held back and lit up a cigar. He listened to the crackle of the red-hot cherry as he inhaled deeply. Checking his gun was loaded, he removed the safety and followed the marauding masses.

The woods echoed with the sound of breaking twigs as the officers, now calmer in their hunt after the initial sprint had put paid to their careless enthusiasm, crept through the undergrowth. Detective Lamb discarded his cigar and peered through the darkness. As his eyes became accustomed to the gloom, he made out the dark shapes of his colleagues moving between the trees and bushes. He was a long way back, but it didn't matter, he suspected where the crazed killer was headed: back to where she killed her boyfriend. For what reason, he did not know. He didn't pretend to understand the thoughts of the deranged, but experience had taught him a lot. Maybe she was going back to fuck his corpse, to worship it, to feast off it.

One thing still puzzled him though. How on earth did she break out of that cell, back at the station?

Lamb needed to clear his mind; to focus on the manhunt. He thought back to his model henge as a means of gaining clarity. The faces of his kids flashed up in his mind, laughing and smiling in the Australian sun; playing with his ex-wife and *him*: their stepfather.

He felt his face screw up in disgust. His hand squeezed the grip of his pistol.

Shots fired up ahead, breaking his tormented reverie; the muzzle flashes lighting up the darkened wood. Detective Lamb ran towards them, encountering his team with their guns aimed in all directions.

'What happened?' he demanded.

'The dogs, sir!' PC Winters shone her torch towards the ground.

Bathed in its spotlight were the two Alsatians, slumped on the floor. Large holes had been ripped through both of them. The wet insides of the animals reflected the light, sparkling in the cold autumn air.

'Briggs has disappeared,' Winters continued.

'Did you see Dunster?' Lamb asked.

'No sir, we're all a little spooked. No one saw a thing,' came her reply.

A scream shattered the tension. As they all turned, they watched PC Roberts drop to his knees in agony. Winters, Lamb, Digby and Davenport trained their spotlights on him as he fell, face forward into the dirt. A jet of bright red blood shot like a geyser from a hole that had been ripped straight through his torso.

The officers fired rounds wildly into the night.

Another scream sounded out over the gunshots. Then another.

The firing halted as Lamb turned and watched Davenport fall onto her back, a hole punched through her stomach. Her innards trailed from her torso, slopping onto the ground with a moist thud.

Digby had already hit the deck by the time Lamb spotted him; his mouth dribbled blood as he tried to breathe, but inevitably failed. His chest had been ripped open, obliterating his ribcage and leaving his punctured lungs looking like slimy scraps of paper as they rasped in time with his failing breath.

Winters and Lamb instinctively stood back to back and began firing again. Without a target they sent shots in all directions, intentionally trying to spread their aim to cover every angle; and only stopping when they had to pause to change clips.

'What the fuck is happening?' Lamb vented as the flurry of gunfire died down, leaving an eerie silence in its wake.

Smoke trailed from their weapons, and their ears rang with the blasts of gunpowder.

'Keep sharp,' Winters replied, her eyes focused forward, scanning the area. 'We've got to nail this creep.'

A movement from the corner of Lamb's eye made him turn; something just above him. As he moved he was struck by an object: hard and sharp. It caught his shoulder, slicing through both his clothes and skin; knocking him to floor. As he landed hard he dropped his gun, losing it to the dark.

Detective Lamb rolled away and looked up to where the attack had come from.

Winters was already on it, her gun aimed and blasting towards the tree tops. Her quick reactions and channelled aggression had served her well in the force but ultimately were of little value here as she screamed into the darkness. The gunshots stopped as her weapon thudded onto the ground. She fell to her knees amidst a squelching sound of torn flesh and broken bone.

Squinting at the downed officer, Lamb could make out a long appendage, like that of a giant insect's leg running through Winters' torso. He followed the leg back up into the trees and was horrified to see it was attached to what looked like Marie Dunster. The unnatural limb, almost six metres in length, protruded from her side, just below her arm. Three other limbs of similar appearance extended from her body – two on each side – and the others gripped onto tree branches, holding her suspended amongst the canopy.

Her eyes glinted in the darkness; almost glowing, but not quite. It was like they were impossibly reflecting the gloom.

He watched her scan the woodland floor, surveying the carcasses, and searching for her prey. Searching for him!

Marie's eyes met his and she clambered towards the detective; her insectoid legs gracefully moving her through the leafless branches.

Lamb got to his feet and ran. His gun had been lost to the undergrowth. Maybe if he could lead her away he could double-back and take a gun from one of his dead colleagues. That is, if he could outrun the monster.

Behind him, he could hear her drawing near, but he didn't dare look back. He had to gain some ground.

Stumbling through the trees, Lamb found himself approaching a clearing, and as he entered the treeless patch he tripped on something and fell. Turning round he saw a tent peg poking from the ground. Yellow crime scene tape flapped in the wind; still tied to the trees surrounding the area, but pulled apart in the middle and left to dangle like plastic streamers. He went to get back to his feet but a shooting pain exploded in his thigh. He looked down to see one of Marie's spider-like appendages thrust deep into his leg, pinning him to where he lay.

As she approached, another one shot forwards, penetrating his shoulder and embedding itself in the dirt below him.

'What's happening to me?' she wailed behind a distorted face. A monstrous mask that had subtly erased her humanity. 'What's going on, Detective Lamb?'

'Marie,' he called to her, trying to talk her down through gritted teeth as he did his best to block out the pain. 'You have to stop this. I don't know what's happening, but we can work it out. We'll get experts to help you.'

'I'm a freak!' she snapped. 'They'll lock me up and poke me with needles. I'll be their curiosity; their lab rat.'

'You're human, Marie. You're a person. You'll have my protection.'

'I don't need your protection. I want to kill you. I want to eat you. And the strangest thing is, I don't care. I don't care about you, I don't care about those dogs and I don't care about Charlie.' She twisted the limb in his thigh, causing the detective to yelp. 'I mean, I should care, but there's nothing inside of me. No sadness, no grief. I feel I should cry. Maybe that would make it all better. But all I have is anger; anger and hunger. All I want to do is destroy.'

'Mari-' his words were cut short as he noticed her attention had been taken by something else.

He turned his head, following the direction of her gaze and in the distance saw a set of lights blinking between the trees.

Marie abruptly pulled her insectoid legs from his wounds, causing the detective to groan with pain. He slowly got to his feet and ambled after her as she crawled through the wood towards the illuminations.

Marie was out of sight in no time, and by the time he reached the crest of the hill he could only guess where she had gone. Not that it needed much guess work.

Below him, at the bottom of the hill and surrounded by ash trees and silver birches was a disc-shaped object. Half of it was buried into the ground, seemingly the result of a heavy impact on landing. The other half rose above the ground at a thirty degree angle; its oval dimensions almost as big as the detective's own house.

Lights of different colour flashed on and off around the side of the disc, producing a kaleidoscopic light show.

Detective Lamb scratched his head as he made his way towards it.

Fuck me, he thought to himself, a goddamned UFO.

The scale of the spaceship could only be fully appreciated when Detective Lamb arrived at the edge of the craft. Its hull was smooth with a rim of lights that impossibly glowed somewhere within its walls, illuminating the darkness of his surroundings with ethereal shades.

As he circled the alien disc, his wonderment eclipsed the fear of Marie Dunster's strange appearance. A glance around, and she was nowhere to be seen. There were no trees to hide amongst within this clearing, and the ghostly glows from the ship meant his vision was not hindered by the witching hour.

Had she gone inside? he wondered.

Eventually, Detective Lamb came across an area of the hull that appeared significantly darker in shade than the rest. Next to it was a pattern of intersecting circles and humming lights. Placing his hand on the pattern he found that by moving his fingers across the lights, he could move them within the circles to create new patterns.

A lock? Some kind of control panel?

It was as good a guess as any, and with curiosity driving him onwards, the detective studied the patterns. What could they mean?

Trying to take control of his racing and jumbled thoughts, Detective Lamb thought back to his model at the station; to allow the calming sensation of precision placing and gluing his miniature clear his mind.

And then it came to him.

The patterns, they looked like the rows in his model; like the circumferences, on which Stonehenge was laid. The lights, could they be the stones? There was even one far enough out for the Heel Stone.

Had these aliens been to Earth before? Was the ancient monument a creation of theirs?

Excitedly following the design and moving the lights into the same positions as the stone circle, Lamb was exhilarated to hear the sound of something mechanical, followed by the darker shade of hull sinking back into the ship and sliding left, allowing an entrance to appear.

A noise from behind, like the soft padding of a galloping horse, made him turn, and just in time. Seeing the twisted form of Marie Dunster sprint towards him on her spider-like limbs, the detective dove away from the craft, just missing her attack by inches.

She thrust another leg at him, and again he threw himself out of harm's way, but not without catching his heel on the sharp claw of her appendage.

By the time he turned to face the monster, she had crawled up onto the UFO and launched herself towards him. Lamb tried to escape but he was in too much pain, and she was too quick.

Pinning him to the ground with her insect legs, Marie towered over her prey with hungry eyes.

Detective Lamb tried to struggle and fight back, but found it impossible to break her grip.

'You can't win,' she growled. 'I am your superior in every way.'

'You killed my friends, you bitch. You broke the law.' He spoke through gritted teeth. 'One way or another I'm taking you in.'

She chuckled with a demonic baritone. 'Are you so committed to the job that you'd die for it?'

'If I have to.'

'But you don't have to. I want to kill you. I want to pull you to pieces and chew on your arteries. But this place – this craft – it's calling me. I owe you a debt for opening it. That debt I will pay with your life.'

'You can't-'

'Do you have children, Detective? Are they not more important than this? Leave now and I will let you live. But if you fight, I will turn you inside out.'

She released her grip and stepped away from him. The detective froze for a moment as he considered his options. She had to pay. She will pay. But right now he had no weapons and a hole through his leg. The odds of defeating this inhuman creature were getting slimmer and slimmer.

He thought back to his kids. To Alex and Noah.

As he slowly stood up, he hobbled towards the darkness of the woods, aware of Marie's gaze on him, but not daring to look at her.

This wasn't over. He would be back. With more officers. And bigger guns.

She would not go unpunished.

But first he needed to get to a hospital. He hoped he'd make it that far before he bled out, alone in this darkened wood.

His exhaustion, sent him to his knees, and amid a strange, forced tranquillity, he pictured the happy smile of his two sons.

The inside of the space craft was dim; poorly lit with a strange red colour being emitted from nowhere obvious. A gentle hum throbbed throughout the corridors as Marie carefully made her way, unsure of where she was heading, but strangely familiar with the things she saw.

Had she visited this place in a dream? Was she dreaming now?

The metal labyrinth was empty except for her, so when she heard the faint sound of someone else it made her jump.

The sound invaded her chest, causing her heart to flutter with excitement. A smile grew across her face as she allowed this odd melody to fill her head. It was the sound of someone crying.

But these weren't just any tears. During her thirst for blood and destruction she'd heard many people cry for their lives. This was different. The melancholy that tickled her ears was the sweetest she'd ever heard; it was wholly satisfying. This was what she had yearned for.

Marie followed the sound until she came to an open door. Steadying herself and summoning the courage to enter, she stepped though the doorway.

Inside, through a layer of fog, she saw a naked female figure strapped to a vertical board, positioned by the far wall. Her head was bowed, looking at the floor as she continued to sob. If the woman had noticed Marie enter she gave no acknowledgement.

Marie walked closer and as the steam grew thinner, she saw three long, thick tubes trailing from inside the woman's vagina, snaking along the wall and ending at the top of a clear dome. Inside the dome, a gel-like substance pulsated and bubbled; spitting like cold water thrown into a hot pan.

Beside the dome lay clear tanks, six foot long and each of them occupied with something of various sizes.

Staring in amazement, she watched the blobs inside the tanks swell and grow. The lid of one opened and the occupant emerged, pulling and clawing at the slimy membrane that surrounded it.

Backing up in shock, Marie watched a pair of familiar hands emerge from the mucus; followed by a nose, a smile, a mane of long, brunette hair. All of these features she knew.

Turning to the woman held captive, Marie gently held her chin and raised her head. Brushing the hair from the prisoner's tear soaked face, Marie looked at herself staring back at her.

The crying continued, even more voraciously.

Confused, a noise behind her caused her to turn.

A creature with three eyes underneath a clear, domed helmet appeared in the doorway. Its scaly hands gripped a cylindrical device that crackled and fizzed at one end.

Jabbing Marie with the weapon, she fell to floor, paralysed by the attack.

The creature began to speak in a strange tongue, yet somehow Marie understood it perfectly.

'Test Spawn One was a success,' it spoke into a device on its wrist. 'Twenty five more have reached maturity; our ranks are swelling. Terminate this one and prepare the army. The invasion begins.'

And so, mere mortal, we must conclude our journey through the dark realms and leave you safely back in the reality you call home. But beware, for now you have entered our world, you can never truly leave. Be cautious of the dark for it has tasted the flavour of your fear; the shadows crave the separation of your flesh and your cries that will undoubtedly accompany their banquet. Goodnight, mortal, may you never sleep again...

Credits

Cover
Art - Jorge Wiles

Inroduction & Featuring Pages
Art - Jorge Wiles

Cernunnos
Story – Daniel Marc Chant

Magic Night
Story – J. R. Park
Art – Mike McGee

Dot To Dot
Created by J. R. Park

Girl Who Kissed The Dead
Story – Tracy Fahey

Word Search
Created by J. R. Park

Sinister Horror Company (Not) Lego
Design, customisation and photogrpahy - J. R. Park
note: the Lego logo is ® of Lego and is used in respectful tribute and for parody purposes.

My Life In Horror: I'll Make You Bleed, As I Did
Written by Kit Power

Stranger
Story – J. R. Park
Anna – Amy Ford
Zoe – Amy Ford
Photography, editing and layout – J. R. Park
Faces:
Page 1, Panel 2
Andrew Lennon, Kit Power, J T Lozano
Page 1, Panel 3
Jonathan Butcher, Naomi Rettig, Shaun Hupp
Page 1, Panel 4
Daryl Duncan, Andrew Freudenberg, Deno Sandz, Stefanie Guest
Page 1, Panel 5
Mike Butler, Zoey Pert, Tara Court, Mortimer Cash, Frankie Yates, Matt Boultby
Page 2, Panel 1
Chris Hall, Gary McMahon, Penny Jones, Fran Comesanas, C. L. Raven
Page 3, Panel 1
C. L. Raven, Brian Asman, Martha-Mai Cash, Dion Winton-Polak, Lex H. Jones,
Steve Matthewman, Chris Barnes, Jamie Dunn
Page 3, Panel 4
Rich Hawkins, Steve J. Shaw, Pippa Bailey, Matty-Bob Cash
Page 3, Panel 5
Mark Adams, Allen Stoud, Zoe Farr, Kasey Hill, Paul Flewitt

White Knuckle Ride
Story – Tim Clayton

The Last Patrol
Story – Andrew Freudenberg

Crash
Story – Lydian Faust
Art – Jorge Wiles
Adapted for comic & Lettering – J. R. Park

Naked Wings
Story – Mark Cassell

Crossword
Created by J. R. Park

The Skirrid Mountain Inn:
A Ghost Hunting Adventure
Written by Kayleigh Marie Edwards

Vengeance
Story & Lettering – J. R. Park
Art – Chris Hall

The Black Room Manuscripts:
Lost Prologue & Epilogue
Story – Duncan P. Bradshaw

Spot The Difference
Created by Stuart Park

Fifty
Story – Chris Kelso

A New Flavour
Story – Jonathan Butcher
Script Advisor – Sian Jansen-Brown
Photography, editing and
story arrangement – David Winter
Mel - Sian Jansen-Brown
Tony – Mark Shorten
Kreb – Jonathan Butcher

The Incredible Case Of Marie Dunster
Story – J. R. Park

Colouring In Page & Outro Page
Art – Jorge Wiles

Sinister Horror Company Logo & Paragraph Break Design – Vincent Hunt

The Sinister Horror Company Annual
Copyright © J. R. Park 2018

Curated, edited and designed by J. R. Park
Published by the Sinister Horror Company

ISBN: 978-1-912578-09-2

Puzzle Solutions

Dot to Dot

The image is the cover to J. R. Park's
Death Dreams In A Whorehouse

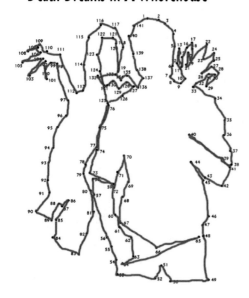

Crossword

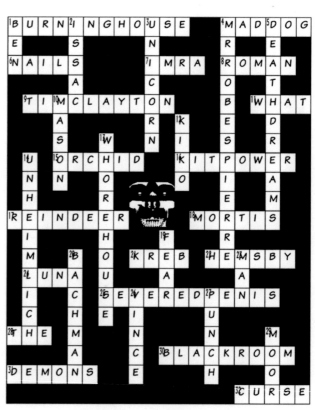

Word Search

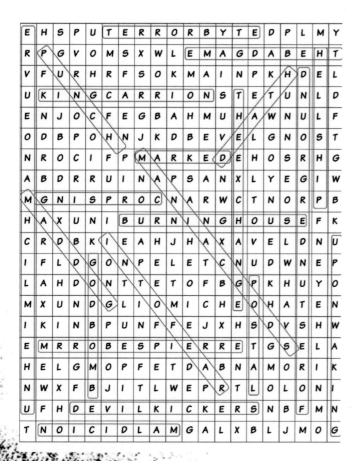

1. Terror Byte
2. The Bad Game
3. Hell Ship
4. Upon Waking
5. Forest Underground
6. Death
7. The Exchange
8. Postal
9. Maniac Gods
10. Burning House
11. Punch
12. The Unheimlich Manoeuvre
13. King Carrion
14. Corpsing
15. Mad Dog
16. Into Fear
17. Marked
18. Godbomb
19. Mr Robespierre
20. Devil Kickers
21. Maldicion

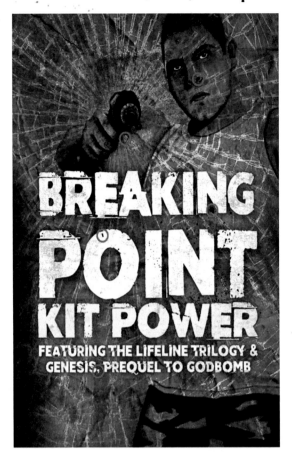

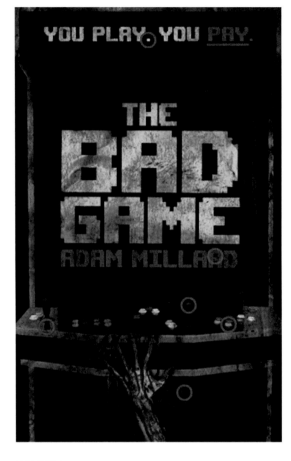

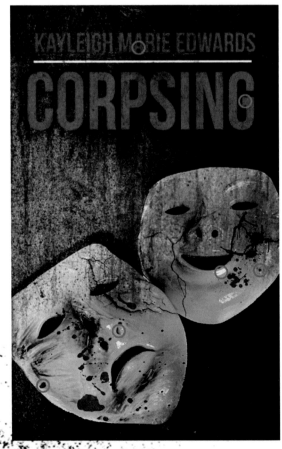

Lightning Source UK Ltd.
Milton Keynes UK
UKRC021259241118
332836UK00005B/161